SHIELDMAIDEN SQUADRON

SHIELDMAIDEN SQUADRON: BOOK ONE

S.T. BENDE

To my little Vikings.
And to Olaug—for sharing a friendship that's timeless.

Shieldmaiden Squadron
Shieldmaiden Squadron: Book One
Copyright © 2021, S.T. Bende
Edited by: CREATING ink
Cover Art by: Melissa Stevens of
The Illustrated Author Design Services
Map by: BZN Studio Designs

First publication: 2021, S.T. Bende

This book is a work of fiction. Names, characters, places, and
incidents either are products of the author's imagination or are used
fictitiously. Any resemblance to actual persons, living or dead,
events, or locales is entirely coincidental.

❄

Meet the demigods in NIGHT WAR SAGA.

PROTECTOR

DEFENDER

REDEEMER

Complete list of S.T.'s licensed children's titles

at https://www.stbende.com/kids-books/

VELKOMMEN TIL VALKYRIS

CHAPTER 1

DON'T MOVE, INGRID. DO. *Not. Move.*

I winced as the business end of a freshly sharpened sword pressed into my neck. The muted, silver blade was cold. And impassive. And unnervingly sharp.

Do. Not. Move.

"Good setup. Now, hold that position." Janna, the captain of the Shieldmaiden Squadron and the fiercest woman I'd ever met, strode across the training room. Her eyes narrowed as she studied my partner. "Eydis, adjust your angle. The tip of your sword should strike Ingrid's neck at forty-five degrees. If you drive in from where you are, you'll hit resistance from her collarbone, and she'll be both upright *and* angry. Not a good combination."

"Understood." My fellow first-year nodded.

"Watch me." Janna stepped back, then raised her

sword to our practice dummy. She kept her blade parallel to the ground as she jammed the tip into the target's neck. Her sword wobbled, but failed to pierce.

Eydis nodded at our leader while I held myself perfectly still so as to avoid potential death-by-impaling. Only my eyes shifted, following Janna's movements and cataloguing each angle for future implementation. Janna had the most battle kills in the history of the Valkyris shieldmaidens. I *so* wanted to be her someday.

"Now, if you adjust that angle *away* from the clavicle, you not only hit an artery and severely debilitate your attacker, but you find minimal muscular resistance if decapitation is your end goal." Janna pulled her arm back and struck the dummy again—this time, at the correct angle. Her sword sliced easily through its neck, and when Janna flicked her wrist to the side, the dummy's straw-stuffed head toppled to the ground. "Everyone follow?"

"Yes, Captain," we chanted in unison.

My arm trembled as I struggled to maintain my position. We'd been running combat sequences for three hours, and while I was usually the last one to tire, my muscles were doubly exhausted from my early morning climbing session. Janna had set up an optional course along the Cliffs of Conquest—the near vertical barrier at the northwest edge of the shieldmaiden compound— and the two of us had scaled it twice before breakfast.

Only the strongest will thrive.

"Is this better?" Eydis raised her elbow so her sword angled toward the hollow of my throat. The tip chilled my skin.

"Much," Janna confirmed. "Ingrid, at ease. You were an excellent target."

"Thanks." I exhaled heavily as I took a step back and lowered my arms. They only trembled a little as the tension ebbed from my triceps.

"That's it for today's practical component. But we will be going over this sequence again, so I want you take your journals home and illustrate the three most optimal kill points, along with the ideal angles of incision. You'll discuss them during practicum tomorrow." Janna holstered her sword, and clapped her hands together. "Squad dismissed. Ingrid, may I have a private word?"

I thought I'd done well enough. Janna must have noticed my fatigue. If she canceled our early morning workouts, I'd lose my edge on the rest of the girls. Falling behind could cost me my spot in Norway's elite female fighting team.

And it was the only place I wanted to be.

"Good luck." Eydis patted my shoulder as she holstered her weapon. "I'll save you a seat at lunch."

"Thanks." I hurriedly wiped down my blade, and did my best to ignore the pitying looks from the other girls as I marched determinedly to the edge of the training ring. Janna was busy reattaching the training dummy's head, so I sheathed my sword and stood at

3

attention with my hands folded at the small of my back.

When the last of the girls had left the room, Janna set the newly re-capitated dummy against the wall and turned to me. "At ease, Ingrid. It's not that kind of talk."

The tension drained from my shoulders. "I know protocol dictates that when in the presence of a superior officer, a—"

"Stop right there." Janna tilted her head so her charcoal braids fell over one shoulder. Her russet-brown skin was pinked from exertion, and drops of sweat trickled down her muscular arms. With her high tolerance for pain and her low tolerance for drama, Janna was an ideal leader. But it was her compassion that made her unique among the high-ranking shieldmaidens. She'd taken me under her wing from the first day of my tryouts, and she'd been my champion ever since.

I honestly didn't know where I'd be without her.

Now she tilted her head and lowered her voice. "I need you to forget protocol for a minute."

"I thought we were *never* supposed to forget protocol. 'Squad above self,' right?"

"Always." Janna nodded. "But in this case, the squad needs you to deviate from routine. I want you to help me with an assignment. And I'm going to need you to lose the whole 'superior officer' mindset to do it."

"Now I'm really confused."

Janna's eyes twinkled. "Let's take a walk."

"Won't you be late for your lunch meeting with the senior—"

4

"Ingrid Tirsdatter. Are you questioning my orders?"

"You just told me to forget protocol."

Janna jutted her chin toward the door. "Outside. Now."

I snapped my heels together, grabbed my cloak from the hook, and followed my captain into the brisk, autumn air. Octobers in southern Norway were usually mild, but today the wind that whipped across the bluffs carried a chill. I hurriedly threw the thick, wool fabric around my shoulders and fastened the cloak's iron clasp at my chest. Janna seemed as unaffected by the weather as she was everything else. Very little rattled her. Whereas me, on the other hand . . .

Well, it had been a rough year.

We walked in silence until we reached the cliffs. Janna paused at the edge, crossing her arms and staring straight ahead. The sea churned below us, its violent grey waves frothing into white-tipped peaks. Above, heavy clouds crowded the sky. We'd need to get inside soon or we'd incur the wrath of Thor. He wasn't hugely forgiving of those who remained outside when he'd given *clear* indicators of a downpour.

"Ingrid." Janna's voice pulled me back.

"Yes?"

"You trust me. Don't you?"

"I'd follow you into any battle any day," I vowed.

Janna turned her head to study me. "But do you *trust* me?"

"I wouldn't follow you into battle if I didn't."

Janna returned her attention to the sea. "What I'm about to tell you is fairly . . . unbelievable."

"Please." I pulled my cloak tighter around me as a fresh gust blew from below. "We live on a magical island in a compound powered by *älva* dust. We have flameless candles, and bucketless baths, and women in governing roles, and, well . . . countless other things I'd never dreamed possible when I moved here last year. Oh, and we have dragons—actual, honest-to-gods *dragons* who work with our airborne assassins to protect our lands. It's safe to say that we're well past *believability*."

"We'll see about that," Janna said drily. She pivoted slowly, squaring her shoulders to mine. "We have a lead on the dark mage who threatened Valkyris a few months' back."

"The same one that brought a dragon back to life?" *And nearly killed us all . . .*

"*Ja,*" Janna said. "We've finally confirmed his location."

My spine straightened. "What are we waiting for? It's our duty to stop him before he hurts anyone else."

And it was. The Shieldmaiden Squadron defended Valkyris' virtues of honor, kindness, and equality, and we ensured no harm came to our island, our chieftains, or our people. Though our colony was protected by magic, we still relied on our warriors to uphold its values and protect the lands beyond our borders from threats.

Even unimaginable ones.

"We *are* going after the dark mage." Janna spoke slowly. "But . . ."

Why is she being so careful?

"Who's on our hunt team? Eydis is young, but she's one of the strongest fighters we've got. Her parents were killed in the northern incineration, and I know she'd gladly give her life if it meant bringing in the mage who destroyed her clan."

"This isn't that kind of mission," Janna said. "You and I are going after the dark mage alone. Well, not exactly alone. We'll have backup. But not from within the squadron."

My eyes narrowed. "But a full unit always goes on kill missions. Squad protocol dictates that no fewer than ten shieldmaidens—"

"I told you we were going to deviate from protocol on this one." Janna met my curious stare. "The mage has been located, but we need to move swiftly before he changes location again."

"Where was he last spotted?"

"After the battle with Clan Bjorn, and the more recent reindeer massacre and incineration of their herders' village, he shifted his focus west," Janna said. "My sources tell me that he crossed the ocean and set up a new camp on the western edge of the landmass beyond Greenland."

I mentally ran through what little I knew about the lands west of ours. My friend Saga and our chieftains' son, Erik, had recently left on a western-heading voyage. "Did Saga and Erik spot him?"

"Highly unlikely," Janna said, "seeing as the dark mage has traveled not only in distance, but also in time."

Wait. *What?*

"Breathe." Janna's hand on my shoulder reined in my panic.

"He can travel *through time?* How the Helheim are we supposed to find him if he's not even where—or when—we are?"

"That's the mission," Janna said calmly. "I need you to be my second as I narrow his location and bring him home. You're the best tracker on the squad—my most dedicated new recruit. And because you've demonstrated an unparalleled level of composure, I know you'll handle this assignment with dignity and decorum."

"Uh, thanks." My fingertips played with the insides of my cloak. "But you didn't answer my question. We can't find someone who's jumped through time. Not unless we . . . I mean, we'd have to . . ."

Janna didn't blink.

Oh. My. Gods.

"No." I shook my head. "No. I cannot believe that."

"You just said we were past believability." Janna's eyes twinkled.

"It is simply not possible for you and I to travel to the past. Or the future. Or . . . whenever. It is *just. Not. Possible.*"

"It is," Janna said simply. "And I'm doing it. Today. Hopefully with you as my second."

"I meant what I said—I'd follow you into any battle any day. But this . . . this is crazy. How is this even . . . how can you . . . can we . . ."

"Chieftess Freia will explain. But I need to know if you're in or out. The transport leaves in one hour. We can't afford to lose the target."

Gulp.

"I'm in," I declared. "You've had my back from my first day here, and I'll always have yours. What do you need me to pack?"

"I've already had weapons and supplies sent to the castle. We're meeting the rest of our team in the chieftains' quarters, and I believe we're porting out from there. This is a top-clearance assignment, which means only Chieftess Freia, Chief Halvar, and the members of our immediate team can know where—and when—we're going."

"Of course." I had one thousand questions, but Janna was already on the move. She marched determinedly along the edge of the cliff, quickly crossing the heather-dusted landscape at the edge of the shield-maiden compound. I hurried to catch up to her, pulling my cloak tighter around my shoulders as we neared the edge of the forest. "We're the only shieldmaidens going?"

"Correct," Janna confirmed.

"Who else is joining us? Warriors? Seers? Do we have access to our own mage?" *Please, let us have our own mage . . .*

"Freia wants a disseminator to document the

9

cultural findings of our new location—and time." Janna looked up as fat droplets descended from the clouds. We quickly broke into a jog.

"That's smart. Maybe we can incorporate new customs on our return. Who else is coming?"

"The disseminator has a protector, apparently—he won't let her go unless he accompanies her. Which may not be a bad thing. My understanding is that he is an extremely competent warrior."

Recognition prickled at the back of my skull. I was aware of only one disseminator with an overprotective warrior companion. My old nemesis, Brigga, had tortured me and my friends during our time at Valkyris Academy. I was none too eager to take a trip with her . . . or with Raynor. The chieftains' younger son hadn't always had our tribe's interests at heart. Raynor had come around in recent months, but I still didn't trust him. Was including him on this mission really the best idea?

"Who else is joining us?" I asked cautiously.

"An assassin," Janna said as she jogged through the forest. "I requested the one with the highest kill rate. As I understand it, he's a favorite of the chieftains. Freia said he'll be a strong asset."

My breath stilled as I ran through Valkyris' catalogue of killers. We didn't have many, and there were even fewer who'd garnered favor from the chieftains. Which meant there was a high likelihood the assassin going on this mission would be . . .

Oh, gods. Please not him.

"Which assassin is coming?" My voice wavered over the words.

"Axel Andersson." Janna didn't break her stride.

Blood drained from my face as I charged after my captain and glared up at the sky.

"Dritt."

CHAPTER 2

"WELL, WELL, WELL. LOOK who's coming on the mission." Axel Andersson, head of Valkyris' Airborne Assassins and all-round pain in my backside, crossed his arms. He stood in the center of the Halvarssons' family quarters, a mug in his hand and a smirk on his face. "You sure you're up to this? You're the only shieldmaiden who didn't grow up on Valkyris. And you *just* joined the squadron, so . . ."

Breathe, Ingrid. Don't let the jerk get to you.

"I'm more than prepared to support my captain in capturing our target and bringing him to justice." I kept my voice calm. "Will that be a problem for you?"

"Not at all." Axel's dimple popped. He set his mug on a table and raked his fingers through the dark brown waves that fell messily around his shoulders. Since he usually tied his hair in a knot, this was one of the first times I'd ever seen it down. It looked good.

Not that I thought Axel looked good. He didn't. I

mean, he didn't *not* look good. I just couldn't appreciate Axel's appearance over his egotistical, narcistic, arrogant—

"Excellent. I see you two have met." Janna stepped into the room behind me.

Axel's emerald eyes crinkled at the corners. He ran his fingertips along the chestnut strands of his neatly trimmed beard. He'd clearly had time to clean up for the mission. Whereas my crimson curls sprung wildly from my braid, and beneath my cloak, my training clothes were still covered in sweat. Axel must have had more notice about our meeting than I had.

Chieftains' pet.

"Ingrid and I go way back," Axel said easily. "Don't we?"

"Yeah. Back to when I saved your sorry butt from Clan Bjorn." I slipped out of my mud-caked shoes and left them by the door before stepping into the pristine space. Freia and Halvar had decorated their family quarters in layers of white, cream, and ivory. And while they both made it clear they valued people above possessions, I didn't want to wreck their living room.

Or give Axel anything to use against me on our mission.

Gods, this is going to be a nightmare.

"Glad you're already acquainted." Janna removed her own shoes, and strode into the living area. "Saves us time on team building. The others should be here any minute. And Chieftess Freia is—"

"I am right here." Freia emerged from a side door,

13

her long blond hair flowing atop her navy robes. I bowed out of habit, and she shook her head with a smile. "No formalities in my home, Ingrid. You know this."

"I do." I righted myself. "Sorry, Chieftess."

"No apologies necessary. It's good to see you." Freia crossed to my side and took my hands in hers. "I'm glad you'll be a part of this mission. When Janna said she wanted to bring you, she had my wholehearted endorsement."

"And mine." Chief Halvar's voice boomed from the doorway. He entered carrying a tray of food, which he set down on a low table. "You've proven a great asset since joining our clan. I have absolute faith that you'll track the perpetrator who's instilled so much fear in the northern territories, and end his reign of terror."

"I'll do my best," I promised. "But Janna said we have to travel to another landmass. Also, to another time? That sounds . . ."

Insane. Impossible. Terrifying.

"Difficult?" Freia offered.

Sure. We'd go with that.

"It will be," Halvar confirmed. He lowered himself into one of the plush, white chairs, and gestured for Janna and I to sit on the couch across from him. "I understand you may have some hesitation. But Freia and I have walked our son through the process. He's familiar with how to use the dagger to transport you to your destination. So long as you follow the instructions, you should have no trouble getting back."

Axel bristled. "Raynor's coming after all?"

"I told you he would be," Freia said gently. "I trust you will *all* look out for one another."

"Of course." Janna sat down.

I quickly followed. "Absolutely."

"We'll see." Axel grunted.

"Axel," Freia admonished. "Raynor is my son."

Axel crossed his arms, and I tried not to notice the way his biceps popped against the fibers of his tunic.

Not the time, Ingrid. And definitely not the guy.

"Regardless." Axel shook his head. "Until recently, his loyalty to your family—and our entire clan—was in question. I won't do anything against him, but I'm only looking out for the women on this mission. They're my priority. Not Raynor."

"Always good to know where I stand." The dry voice came from behind me.

I looked over my shoulder to find Raynor leaning against the front door. He pushed off, then bent to remove his boots. Droplets fell from his hair with the movement.

"There are linens near the bench." Freia pointed. "I take it the storm has commenced?"

"It's definitely coming down." Brigga, my onetime-nemesis turned first-year disseminator, followed Raynor through the door. She nodded to the chieftains' son before handing him one of the thick towels Freia kept in the entry. "Did you hear the thunder? Thor is angry today."

"I hope that's not true. We need to move swiftly."

Freia lifted the kettle from the table, and filled two of the waiting cups with steaming liquid. "Halvar, fetch me more mugs, will you?"

"Of course, my love." Our chief rose from his chair. He pulled several cups from the cabinet by the fireplace, and set them in front of his wife.

"*Takk.*" Freia continued pouring while Brigga toweled the moisture from her long, blond hair. She removed her cloak and hung it by the door before following Raynor into the sitting area. I scooted closer to Janna to make room for her on the couch.

"Ingrid." Brigga nodded.

"*Hei,*" I responded cautiously. Brigga had changed a lot since our days at Valkyris Academy. But it had only been a few months since we'd graduated, and I didn't know how lasting that change would be. Experience had taught me to keep a healthy distance from . . . well, *everyone.* At least until trust could be assured.

Which, with Brigga, was probably *never.*

"Raynor." Janna bowed her head as the Halvarssons' second son settled into the chair beside her. Raynor's older brother, Erik, was currently on a cross-sea journey with my friend Saga. Erik could be intimidating, but at least I'd always known where I stood with him. Whereas Raynor . . .

Is this seriously our mission team?

"Good to see you, Janna." Raynor took the cup from his mother. "Congratulations on your promotion. The shieldmaidens are in capable hands."

"I'm grateful to serve our chieftains." Janna placed

16

her fist over her heart before turning to her right. "And you must be our disseminator."

"I'm Brigga." She reached across me to shake Janna's hand. "Good to meet you."

"This is Axel." Janna gestured to the still-scowling assassin standing behind his own chair.

"Axel and I are . . . well acquainted." Brigga bit on her bottom lip.

Blech.

Halvar's brows arched, no doubt in response to the awkward tension now pinging between Brigga and Axel. I ignored them all, and set my sights on my chieftess. "What exactly is our assignment? Janna only had a few minutes to brief me."

"That's because this excursion requires the utmost discretion." Freia finished handing out the mugs before crossing to the cabinet near the window. She opened the hutch and retrieved a small dagger. She examined its handle before returning to her seat and laying the dagger flat across her lap. "What I'm asking you to do has never before been attempted in the history of Valkyris. Or the world, so far as I am aware. I need you to track the dark mage who's been assaulting our lands. And I need you to track him in his current location . . . five thousand miles to the west, and one thousand years in the future."

"Consider it done," Axel said easily.

Gods, could he be any more arrogant?

"How exactly are we to track the mage?" Janna asked.

"And how are we going to travel five thousand miles?" Raynor leaned forward. "Our sturdiest ships have only traveled a portion of that distance."

"You'll track him using this." Halvar held up a small, clear vial. Inside swirled a golden mist. "It's an *älva*-enchanted trace. Release it within range of the mage, and it will form a direct trail to his location."

"What's considered within range?" I asked.

"We're not entirely sure." Halvar glanced at his wife. "A few miles? Possibly more."

I reached across the table, and took the vial from my chief. "How does it work?"

"We aren't certain of that, either," Halvar admitted. "A Valkyris warrior collected a piece of the mage's cloak and delivered it to our *älva* handlers. They were able to use the faerie's magic to create this trace. But they cautioned it could have only one application—to create a second trace, they'll need another sample."

"And since the mage has already time jumped, that's out of the question," Janna deduced. "Unfortunate."

"Use the trace well, and you won't need a second dosage," Halvar said. "But just in case, I'm sending a satchel of *älva* dust along with you. Keep it safe—we don't know whether the future world is accustomed to magic. And we don't know what the dark mage would do with it if it were to fall into his hands."

"Thank you." I took the offered satchel and tucked it into the pouch at my waist. "I'll guard this with my life."

"As this mission's tracker, I hope you'll find it useful in acquiring the target," Halvar said. "I cannot impress upon you how urgent this matter has become. In addition to threatening our own world, the mage now threatens the future."

"About that." Brigga glanced at Raynor. "How are we supposed to *get* to the future?"

Raynor lobbed the question to Freia. "You're actually letting us use it?"

"Use what?" I asked.

"This." Frigga raised the dagger from her lap. Its silver blade bore runic etchings, and its handle held several sparkling gems. Or were they crystals? My friend Helene had used crystals in her healing coursework. She'd said certain stones had properties similar to *älva* dust. But not even magic rocks could transport us to the future.

Could they?

Freia glanced at Halvar. "It has recently come to our attention that the dagger we used to establish Valkyris is capable of more than we believed."

"Like time travel?" Axel arched one brow.

"Like time travel," Freia confirmed. "After this briefing, provided the storm allows it, I will take you to our island's sacred site. There, you will use this blade to transport yourselves to the target's location and time. Ingrid, you will track him. Janna and Axel, you will contain him. And Raynor, you will ensure no one loyal to him remains behind. We want anyone associated with the target returned to present-day Valkyris, where they will be put to trial and held accountable for their crimes against the territories—both current and future."

Janna and I exchanged worried looks. Exactly what was happening in the world . . . or worlds?

"What do you want me to do?" Brigga asked quietly.

"You are to serve as the mission's disseminator," Freia said gently. "Document your findings—the tools our brothers and sisters in the future use, the foods they eat, their family structures, their concept of art, literature, sports. Bring this information directly to me on your return, and we will go over it together. Whatever we deem to be of use in our current way of life we will share with the disseminators for distribution throughout the territories. And information we believe our people might not be ready to receive we will set aside."

Brigga's eyes widened. "You want me to help you make those decisions?"

"My son trusts you," Freia said with a smile. "Therefore, so do I."

My gaze shifted to Axel.

He stood silently, his eyes darting around the room. "Is there anything else we should know?" Axel's voice bore his characteristic calm. But he'd been my combat trainer during my academy days, and I'd worked with him enough to guess that his warrior brain was probably already running through scenarios.

"Only that the mage was last spotted within an educational facility," Halvar answered. "From what we've gathered, this academy is near a center of commerce whose considerable population espouses values largely different from those we uphold in Valkyris."

"How so?" I asked.

Freia folded her hands over the dagger's hilt. "As we understand, citizens there are less willing to help one another than those in our land. You may not find much assistance in locating your charge."

"That won't be a problem," Janna said confidently. "Ingrid's the top of her year in traces, both organic and non-organic. She's proven herself to be our most valuable tracker—her accuracy exceeds even senior-level shieldmaidens."

Heat flooded my cheeks.

"Is that so?" Axel turned his laser-focus on me. "Not bad, shieldmaiden."

I forced myself to hold his stare. "Thank you."

"You may also find it difficult to assimilate your surroundings," Halvar continued. "But I trust that you'll work together to return the target—and any co-conspirators—to Valkyris with utmost urgency. Axel, Raynor, and Brigga, my wife and I have packed the supplies we believe you'll need for your journey. And Janna, I understand you've had weapons sent over for yourself and Ingrid."

"That's correct," Janna confirmed.

"Excellent." Halvar stood. "Time really is of the essence. If there are no further questions, we should get to the extraction site."

I studied my team warily as I followed Halvar to the

door, then suited up to go outside. Besides Janna, there wasn't anyone in this group I wanted to embark on *any* mission with—much less one that would take us thousands of miles—*and* years—from home. Raynor was a loose crossbow, Brigga's loyalties were questionable at best, and Axel was . . . well . . .

My eyes narrowed as the assassin held the door open and motioned for me to step through.

When I hesitated, he leaned down to whisper in my ear. "Top tracker, eh? Sounds like I trained you well."

"You trained me in combat," I lobbed. "Don't flatter yourself."

Axel chuckled as he followed me out of the door. "Bad day, shieldmaiden?"

"I'm about to take a thousand-year journey with *you*," I hissed as we marched past the warriors who stood guard in the hallway outside the Halvarssons' suite. "How do you *think* I'm feeling?"

Axel smirked. "Most girls would be thrilled."

"Yeah, well. I'm not most girls." I lengthened my stride, swerving around Brigga so I moved in next to Freia. "Where exactly did you say we're going?"

"To the west, roughly five thousand miles." Freia glanced at the dagger as she rounded a corner, and hastened down the stairs. "A coastal town called . . . Los Angeles."

"Los Angeles." I turned the strange name around in my head. "I wonder what it's like."

"If it's coastal, it must be similar to the seafaring villages we have here." Janna fell in step behind us.

"Shipping, fishing, trade ports . . . the usual oceanside vocations will likely hold through time. Things can't have changed *that* much. Can they?"

I looked over my shoulder, ignoring the glares Axel and Raynor now traded.

Boys.

"I have no idea." I returned my attention forward. "But we're about to find out."

CHAPTER 3

T IME TRAVEL PROVED TO be absolutely terrifying. It only took a few minutes to reach the sacred spot—a heather-lined patch of dirt atop the bluffs overlooking the western edge of our island. Janna, Brigga, and I each gripped a prong of the dagger's hilt, while Axel and Raynor placed their palms alongside opposite edges of its blade. Freia raised her hands to the sky, her voice piercing the storm as she sang an incantation. In my pouch I carried a piece of parchment with the words we'd need to recite to return home. Before beginning the ritual, Freia had explained that using the dagger would activate some kind of inner-ear translator, so we'd be able to speak the language wherever we landed. And she'd stressed that we were *not*, under any circumstances, to lose the dagger. Not only was it our passage home, but it was the very heart of our island. Without it, Valkyris could very well cease to exist.

No pressure.

Rain pelted us from all sides, the wind switching course as Freia finished her song. Janna had ordered our shields be delivered along with our weapons, and I was pretty sure the large, wooden disk on my back was the only thing keeping my supply pack from getting completely soaked. As instructed, I tried to imagine our destination. *Los Angeles*. The name still sounded strange, so I pictured the coastal town I was most familiar with—my home village, located in the far north.

My life in Clan Firense hadn't been particularly happy. That tribe was ruled by a chief who'd turned a blind eye to my father's mistreatment of me and my mother, and allowed countless other males to treat their families however they pleased. But it was the only sea village I knew, so I focused on the memory of its docks, fishing boats, and the longhouse that sat atop its cliffside village center. As I recalled the smell of freshly baked lefse, the world in front of me wavered out of focus. I sucked in a breath as Axel's face blurred, then spun in a dizzying circle that sent my stomach into a freefall.

What was happening? And how the Helheim was I supposed to stay upright with the ground whirling out from under my feet?

Axel stared at me from across the huddle. His eyes widened, concern lining his normally relaxed features. The trajectory of our spin increased, and his eyes lost their characteristic sparkle. His lightly tanned face paled several shades. My gut churned as the sea behind us blurred into a blue-grey blob. Through the haze I could make out three distinct things: the flash of lightning that burst through the nearly black clouds; the weight of the dagger against my palm; and Axel Andersson's hand holding tight to my forearm. For reasons I *really* didn't want to examine, I took a small amount of comfort in the knowledge that whatever was coming, I'd be facing it with my onetime trainer.

And Janna, Brigga, and Raynor.

My arm shook as the ground disappeared completely. The dagger let loose with a series of fierce, rhythmic pulses. I raised the hand not holding its hilt and placed it atop Axel's. He released his grip on my arm and laced his fingers through mine. We held on tight as the world around us disappeared. We were sucked into an all-white void, and swathed in a cloak of silence.

My throat clenched as I stared at the four faces surrounding me. We floated—literally floated—in a sea of nothingness. Raynor's already pale skin bore a greenish tint, Brigga's eyes were wide with panic, and Janna's normally stoic face had formed an expression bordering on fear. Axel, to his credit, held my gaze with a look that seemed to say, 'I've got you.'

If I was going to die in this void, I'd be dying with the assassin who'd first taught me to fight. It was ironic, really.

A sudden *POP* filled the air, and the void was replaced by an unfamiliar landscape. My feet hit a ground that was harder than any back in Valkyris, and certainly not one covered in the sand or pebbles I'd expected of a beach. Either we'd missed Los Angeles, or coastal towns had changed *a lot* in one thousand years. In fact, there was no coast anywhere to be seen—there wasn't so much as a drop of water, save for the fountain that stood ten yards in front of me. There certainly wasn't a beach, or any boats, or anywhere for these villagers to fish. There were, however, plenty of trees. None like those back home, but tall ones with jagged rectangles of bark pointing upward along their trunks and a small tuft of leaves fanning down from their tops. Buildings stood behind the trees—massive, multistoried buildings that rose from the hard-surfaced ground and glistened in the late afternoon light.

Or was it early morning?

The sun was low in the sky, but it shone through a thick haze that obscured what seemed to be mountains in the distance. As I willed my stomach to settle, I refocused my attention on my team. Raynor's skin had returned to its normally pale pallor, Brigga looked slightly less panicked, and Janna's stoic mask was firmly back in place. Each of them released their hold on the dagger before stepping back and drawing their weapons. Before we'd left, Freia had tasked me with keeping the dagger safe, and I now shoved it into the sheath on my belt. Then I snapped its cover into place to obscure it from view. It wasn't until I reached for my sword that I looked down. I was still holding tight to Axel's hand.

As I stared at our entwined fingers, he leaned over to whisper in my ear. "You all right?"

"I'm fine." My voice wavered. "That was . . . rough."

"No *dritt*," he murmured. "But we should—"

"*Ja.* Obviously." I ripped my hand from Axel's, and pulled my sword from its holder. With my other hand, I drew my shield from around my back and held it in front of my chest. Whatever this place was, we'd close ranks until we knew we were secure.

Shieldmaiden safety, 101.

"We're too exposed on this walkway. Reconvene in that . . . extremely small forest." Janna jutted her chin at the tiny patch of grass with a hard, grey path winding through it. The little square contained trees spaced at strategic intervals and a row of benches. Structures lined three sides, with the fourth open to a wider, ash-colored road. It was the strangest forest I'd ever seen.

"Move out," Axel ordered.

We lowered our weapons and ran for the shelter of the trees. When we'd reached the grass, we stood together, our backs in a tight circle while we scanned our surroundings.

"Assessment protocol," Janna said sharply. "Identify immediate threats. Ingrid?"

"A half-dozen civilians seated beneath a tree at my two o'clock," I reported. I studied the strangely dressed group, each of whom stared blankly at a small box in their hands. A sign behind them read *Spartan Park,* and I quickly logged it as a mental place-marker in case I got separated from the group. "Additional villagers are moving in the distance, though none are currently approaching our unit. And none appear to be armed."

"Axel?" Janna barked.

"Structures obscuring visibility." On my right, Axel knocked his bow. "Possible rooftop assailants, though none presently detected. Note the presence of reflective windows—it's impossible to determine whether they have warriors in attack positions inside."

"Keep your arrows ready," Janna advised. "Raynor?"

"The skies are clear," Raynor confirmed from behind me. "If they have airborne units, their dragons are currently inactive. Or cloaked."

"They can cloak their dragons here?" Brigga whispered.

"No way to tell," Raynor said grimly. "Be prepared to defend yourself."

"That's the plan." Brigga gritted her teeth.

"Any sign of the dark mage?" Janna asked.

"No." Axel shifted so his bow pointed at the building to my left. "But seeing as none of us have made direct contact with him, we don't exactly know what to look for."

"Adult male, looks to be roughly twenty-five years old, with dark hair. That's all I have to go on." I scanned the region again, noting the approach of ten additional civilians from the walkway near the fountain. "He could be anyone. Or anywhere."

"We need to gather more intel," Janna declared. "Freia said we'd be dropped at the time and coordinates of his last-known location. Which means he can't be far from here—or now. If we release the tracking essence, maybe it can—"

BING! BONG! BONG! BONG!

I jumped at the chimes echoing from the tall, red tower to my left. Axel immediately crooked his bow at its ivy-laced sides.

"Sounds like the bell that signaled our class changes at Valkyris Academy," he noted.

"The same bell also signals our call to arms in the event of attack." I dropped into a fighting stance. "Maybe we triggered some kind of alarm, and their warriors are about to—"

"Oh, gods. Look." Brigga's elbow nudged my back. I turned around, then followed the line of her pointed finger to the walkway. Dozens of civilians—or possibly undercover warriors—strode along the hard, ash-colored path. Some wore satchels on their backs, others carried books in their arms, and while a handful chatted happily, most kept their eyes on the small boxes in their hands. Whatever those things were, they seemed to be of great importance to the citizens of Los Angeles.

"Whoa! Epic cosplay. Can I take a selfie?" The unfamiliar voice came from behind me.

"Stand down," Axel barked.

I spun around to find Axel's arrow aimed at a chest. Its owner looked to be our age, with shaggy blond hair, wide brown eyes, and an expression that bordered on curiosity and contempt. At Axel's urging, he raised his arms in the air. His right hand clutched one of the small, rectangular boxes.

"Easy, dude. Shakespeare in the Park doesn't start until six. You guys are early."

Axel didn't lower his weapon.

"Shakespeare in the Park?" I asked.

"Yeah. Today's performance is one of the comedies, right? *Twelfth Night?*"

Performance?

My eyes darted to the sign by the bench. *Spartan Park.* Right. He must have thought we were here to put on some kind of a play. I didn't know what a Shakespeare was, but we had a drama department back at the academy. Its students performed the sagas that told the stories of our history. Apparently, that tradition would survive the next thousand years.

"Sweet." The boy leaned closer. "Is that a real arrow? Last year you had those fake, plastic ones."

I reached over and lowered Axel's weapon with my sword. "Sorry about him. He takes performing *very* seriously."

"What are you doing?" Axel hissed at me.

"My job," I whispered back. "He's a civilian. Freia said to blend."

"She also said to stay alive." Axel's eyes darted to the boy's hand. "And he's holding a weapon."

"I don't think it is. They all have them. See?" I nodded at the group still sitting by the bench. Each stared blankly at their own small, rectangular box.

"You know I can hear you, right?" The boy rolled

his eyes, and raised the device. It reflected our images back at us, like some kind of a tiny, glowing mirror. "So, can I take a selfie or what?"

Janna shifted at my left. She leaned forward to study the box. "Is that a detonator?"

My gods. My team was the worst at this.

"Of course you can take a selfie," I said. I didn't know what that was, but the boy spoke the word so casually, the only reasonable answer seemed to be in the affirmative.

"You're not taking anything from us." Raynor didn't lower his broadsword.

The boy looked as if we'd all gone mad. "Never mind. I have class anyway." He rolled his eyes and turned toward the walkway. As he stormed away he muttered, "Theatre geeks."

"That went well," Raynor said confidently. "We've successfully deflected our first potential assailant. Now we just need to track the target and—"

"Argh!" Brigga shrieked as a metal contraption careened along the walkway. It had four wheels, open sides, and carried two civilians behind a clear, glass window. "What is that thing?"

"A . . . wagon?" Janna guessed.

"A horseless wagon?" Axel raised his bow again. "How does it run?"

"Same way our bucketless baths do, I guess." I squinted at the contraption, which beeped as it wove between the civilians. "Magic."

"They have magic here, too?" Brigga exhaled. "Thank gods."

"They must." Raynor craned his neck. "I knew we should have brought a dragon."

"Freia said dragons would stand out," Janna reminded him.

"She was wrong," Raynor said. "They have them. Look."

A thunderous roar echoed overhead, and I tilted my head back. A large, metallic beast soared across the haze. It left a stream of white smoke in its wake as it crossed the sky at breakneck speed. "That's what their dragons look like?"

"Apparently," Axel muttered.

This place was bizarre.

"We need to find shelter," Janna reminded us. "The civilians appear to be on a unified trajectory—like our cattle at feeding time. If we follow them, they may lead us to their dwellings. We can make camp there, and plan our next steps."

I nodded at my captain. "We should sheathe our weapons. Nobody else is carrying one."

"They all have detonators." Raynor pointed his sword at the crowd.

"I think they're mirrors. Or selfies. I'm not sure what they call them." I shrugged. "Either way, we need to disappear in the crowd or the mage will know we're here. We can't tip our hand before we've had the chance to make a plan."

"Agreed." Axel shouldered his bow. "But I'm shooting at the first sign of trouble."

"Fair enough." I stepped back onto the path. "Let's move."

My team joined me on the smooth surface, and we followed the crowd past the fountain. Despite our weapons, and the fact that none of the civilians wore cloaks, tunics, or the leather pants we donned for training days, nobody paid us much attention. The villagers' own clothes spanned a breadth of styles, from short skirts to loose pants to, in the case of one girl, an all-black lace ensemble that looked like something a sorceress might wear. Each of them was focused on either their walking partner or their handheld box, which meant that no one made eye contact with my team. Maybe blending in would be easier than I'd thought.

We walked for a few minutes before we reached a crossing. Horseless wagons raced along a black trail with twin stripes down its center. They slowed only when the string of overhead lights shifted from green to yellow. When yellow turned to red, the crowd surged forward. I inched closer to Janna's side as we were thrust onto the throng.

"Careful," she warned. "These horseless wagons are bigger than the one we saw before. And they move much faster."

Raynor bent as he walked, rapping his knuckles on the nearest wagon. "They're made of some kind of metal," he deduced. "Impact at high speed would be lethal. Steer clear when they're operating at—"

"What the hell!" The wagon's rider poked his head out of the window. "Don't touch my car, freak!"

Car. I catalogued the word, and pushed the now-bristling Raynor forward.

"Sorry," I called. "Won't happen again."

"It better not, or I'll sue your sorry a—"

The blare of a horn interrupted the villager's vow, and we hurried across the trail as the cars leapt forward. They barreled along the black surface, leaving my team and I staring at the bevy of transports unlike any we'd seen before.

"The horseless wagons are called cars," I stated. "And their owners seem very possessive of them."

"I'm already drafting my report." Brigga shook her head. "What kind of coastal village is this?"

"Maybe the sea is up ahead." I pointed along the walkway. "Near the residences the civilians must be going to."

"That makes sense." Axel nodded. "But they're likely to have more warriors guarding their settlement. I'll take point. Raynor, guard the girls from the back."`

"We don't need guarding." I elbowed my way past Axel. "*I'll* take point. Axel, watch my flank."

"I outrank you," he reminded me.

"And *I* outrank *you*, Andersson." Janna's voice was firm. "Ingrid, take point. Axel, don't mess with my shieldmaiden."

Axel sighed, but did as Janna instructed. I tried not to smirk as the arrogant assassin fell in behind me. We continued along the walkway in a tight huddle, passing twin rows of structures that appeared to house a multitude of residents. Patches of grass stood between the buildings and low, wooden fences, behind which a bevy of boys—all seeming to be our age—tossed discs and drank from red cups. This must have been the males' quarters. Maybe these were their off-duty warriors. Which meant the females' quarters must have been up ahead.

"We need to secure lodging," Janna reiterated. "And we need to map out our plan. If we can locate the village chieftains, we might be able to ask for shelter, and ascertain the last known location of the dark mage."

I paused in front of a particularly large building. It was all white, with three levels of windows and a massive, tiled roof. An enormous lawn stretched between the structure and the walking path, and though it lacked towers or turrets, this was clearly a castle. It had to be—it was the largest home in the vicinity.

"I think Los Angeles' chieftains live in here," I announced. "We just need to request an audience, and—"

"Oh, my god, Becky. Would you look at their costumes? They're *so* ready for tonight's Halloween party!"

"I told you we should have done Viking. It's *soooo* in right now."

36

My palm flew to the hilt of my sword as two giggling girls descended the white castle's steps. Both were dressed in skirts so short they only just covered their backsides, and tightly fitted sweaters that barely contained their ample bosoms. They wore their long hair down, and tottered toward us on shoes with spiked heels that seemed highly unsuitable for combat.

Obviously, these weren't the village's battle maidens.

Axel stepped forward. "Well, *hei* there."

"My god, Lexi! He's even got a bow and arrow! The Alphas have *totally* outdone themselves on the party theme." The taller of the girls tossed her loose, brunette curls over one shoulder before sauntering toward Axel. Her hips moved back and forth with such exuberance, her skirt nearly exposed her nether regions. Who the Helheim dressed like this?

"Hi." The brunette exhaled breathily. She reached up with one crimson fingernail to stroke Axel's beard. "I'm Becky. And you must be the new exchange student in the Alpha house."

"Huh?" Axel's eyes glazed over. Whether from stupidity, or because Becky's nail had shifted and was now making a downward trajectory along his chest, I couldn't be sure.

"The exchange students who are moving into the Alpha house." Becky stepped closer, so her chest pressed against Axel's. "You're from Norway, right?"

"Uh ..."

"Yes," I replied. Busty Becky had unknowingly given

us the perfect cover . . . so long as Axel didn't blow it. "We're the exchange students from Norway."

"We?" Becky's eyes narrowed. "No. Kappa Mu regional told us our exchange students had canceled— they decided to study at the University of Hawaii."

"You received bad information," Janna said smoothly. "We're here. Exchange studenting, um, here. At Los Ang-uh-leese."

Becky narrowed her eyes. "At Southern California State, you mean?"

"Yes. There. Here." I nodded. "With the Alphas."

Behind Becky, Lexi crossed her arms. "The Alphas are a fraternity. For *boys*."

Oh. Right.

"Ingrid means that Axel and I are exchange studenting with the Alphas." Raynor jumped in. "She, Brigga, and Janna are exchange studenting with you. The home for girls."

"Kappa Mu," Becky said skeptically.

"Yes." Janna stared Becky down. "Kappa Mu."

From the girls' dubious expressions, we weren't exactly selling ourselves. But they'd bought that we were foreign, which hopefully gave us some kind of a language-barrier pass.

Internal translators could only get us so far.

"Oh my god, are you our sisters from the University of Oslo?" a high-pitched voice trilled from the porch. A girl bounced up and down, her silky black hair gleaming in the afternoon light. She wore the same tight sweater as her castle-mates, but hers seemed to have frayed—it stopped just above her bejeweled belly button.

How did they fight in these clothes?

"You guys, get down here! The Norwegian girls are here! And oh, my god, did you bring boys with you?"

Axel's chest puffed, and I delivered another elbow to his side. "Warrior up, Andersson. You're the one who told us to look out for threats."

"Do they look threatening to you?" Axel pointed at the stream of girls now pouring through the front door. They descended on us in an enthusiastic horde, chattering excitedly about what they perceived to be our costumes, my curls, and of course, Axel's muscles.

Typical.

"Welcome, sisters." The black-haired girl clasped my hands between hers. "We're so glad you came. We thought you'd decided to go to Hawaii!"

"Yes, well." I shot Janna a look. "We couldn't pass up the opportunity to meet our, uh, sisters at . . ."

"Southern California State," Janna finished smoothly. "I'm Janna, and this is Ingrid and Brigga."

"I'm Kayla Takahashi." The girl squeezed my hands. "President of Kappa Mu, Los Angeles, and international representative to the Panhellenic Council. It is my honor to welcome you to our chapter, and to host the three of you for the remainder of the school year."

"Host us?" My brows shot to my hairline. "You mean we get to stay here?"

"Of course." Kayla tilted her head. "Didn't they

explain that in your transfer papers? Oh, no. You don't have a house off-campus, do you? We have a room all ready for you—we'd cleared it before we heard you weren't coming, and we were *so* hoping you'd live with us."

"What about them?" I tried to point to Axel and Raynor, but Kayla hadn't released her hold on my hands.

"The guys? They're from the University of Oslo's Alpha chapter, aren't they?" Kayla beamed. "The Alpha house is next door. The two-story Tudor with the lions out front."

I glanced over Kayla's head. Sure enough, a brown-beamed estate stood just beyond the girls' white castle. How many palaces did this village have?

"They live in gender-specific castles," Brigga whispered. "Assimilation requires we separate."

My eyes met Axel's. His impervious nod let me know he agreed with this plan.

"Very well," Janna announced. "The, uh, guys will go to the Alpha house. And we will stay here. With you. In this castle."

"It *is* like a castle, isn't it?" Kayla trilled. "Awesome! Don't worry about your guys. We'll see them at the Halloween party tonight. The one you're already dressed for. Way to show up prepared. Go you!"

The girls behind Kayla giggled in seeming approval.

"Where's your luggage?" a fellow redhead asked. "We'll help you bring your bags in."

"Oh, we traveled light," Janna said.

"You came all this way and you don't have any bags?" Becky narrowed her eyes. "That's weird."

"We have everything we need," I said easily. "And I'm sure you can help us procure anything we've forgotten."

"Of course we will," Kayla enthused. "We're your sisters! Our casa is your casa."

Whatever that meant.

"Now, get inside!" Kayla finally released my hands, and shooed me toward the front door. "We can't wait to show you your room! We even themed it for you. I hope you like Elsa!"

I glanced over my shoulder as I was shepherded toward the white structure. "Axel. We need to—"

"It's okay," he assured. "Get settled. We'll reconvene tonight and discuss . . . that thing."

"But . . ." How did we talk about our mission without all of these girls picking up on it? "Time is of the essence."

"And so is securing shelter," Janna whispered in my ear. "It's all right. The leader said we'd reconvene with our 'guys' tonight."

Fine.

"Goodbye, Axel, Raynor," I called out. "We'll meet up with you later. At . . . uh . . ."

"The Halloween party at the Alpha house!" Kayla called. "Eight o'clock! See you then!"

Raynor nodded. "We'll be there."

"Wouldn't miss it." Axel winked. His grin deepened as Lexi and Becky walked past him, their hips swishing unnaturally. Either they had issues with their joints, or they were determined to hook our men.

Not that I cared. I had far more pressing concerns to worry about.

Like how I was going to convince a castle full of girls that I belonged here—and now. And that my outfit was some kind of a costume. And that I *wasn't* here to track a dark mage and send him one thousand years into the past, before he destroyed everything we all knew and loved.

I definitely had my work cut out for me.

CHAPTER 4

"OH, MY GOD, WE are *so* excited you're here. Our social calendar totally filled up the minute we announced we were hosting Kappa Mus from Norway. *All* the frats wanted exchanges with us. Seriously, pretty much every Thursday and Friday night are booked, from here until Christmas." Kayla practically bounced as she led us into a grand foyer. It was similar to the one in the castle back home, but on a smaller scale. A massive chandelier dripping in flameless candles hung over a round table that held a sparkly vase of flowers. A sitting room stood to the right, with couches, chairs, and walls lined with books. A hallway on my left led to a series of rooms. I craned my neck to peer into the nearest one, where a group of girls sat hunched over books—this must have been their library. A split staircase stood directly in front of me, switching directions at the shiny, stained-glass window bearing the image of a fleur-de-lis. Around the symbol were the words *friendship, sisterhood,* and *charity*. This must have been their creed. Which would make this organization . . . a squadron? Were these girls Los Angeles' shield-maidens?

If so, where was their weapons vault?

"Okay. So, Meri—she's our social chair—will get you copies of our events calendar. It's a good one this semester—parties, bowling nights, philanthropies. It might be a little more intense than what you guys did back in Oslo—I'm not sure how big your Greek system is there, but—"

"You're Greek?" I blinked at Kayla. "I thought you were Los Angelenians."

"Los Angeleeeses," Janna corrected.

"Los Angelinos," Kayla chimed in. "And some of us are. I think Helen is half—her dad's from Athens. But most of us are from other places—Nor Cal, Texas, Washington. Meri's a transfer from Minnesota."

"Too cold there." A striking blonde rubbed her bare arms, miming a shiver.

I frowned. "I thought you just said you were Greek?"

"I meant the Greek *system*," Kayla clarified. Her eyes shifted between our blank stares. "Sororities and fraternities. The houses like this and the Alphas and, well, all the ones on this street. Is it called something else where you're from?"

"Oh. The *Greek* system," Janna said quickly. "Sorry. Sometimes we're a little slow with the, uh, language."

"Your English is *way* better than my Norwegian," Meri said kindly. "*Jeg kan snakker litt Norsk*, but pretty much only to ask where for *vafler* on Syttende Mai."

"I *love* waffles," I enthused. "I've got an amazing recipe I'll teach you."

"I hope it involves Nutella." Meri grinned.

What the Helheim was Nutella?

"Of course," I improvised. "It's the best . . . erm, ingredient?"

Please, Nutella, be an ingredient.

"Absolutely. Don't tell my grandmother, but sometimes I put it on my lefse instead of cinnamon-sugar-butter. I'll trade her recipe for yours—it's to die for. And it uses instant potatoes, so it's *super* easy to make." Meri hooked her arm through mine, and led me toward a wide doorway. Through it was a room covered in white linen-topped tables, and a countertop that looked into a vast cooking space. "Our kitchen and dining areas are in here. Monday night dinners start at six, and we wear black cocktail dresses. It's kind of chaotic, but definitely fun—pledges from the different houses deliver announcements and messages. Chapter meetings are held afterwards, beginning at seven-thirty. It's probably not that different from what you did back home."

"Yes," Janna nodded sagely. "We had the same back in Oslo. Though as we packed light, we didn't bring our, um, cocktail dresses."

"That's okay. We have a castaway closet. And if you can't find something in there, you can borrow anything from me," Kayla enthused. "Ingrid, you're about my size. Meri, think anyone might be a match for Janna and Brigga?"

"We'll take care of you," Meri assured. "Sisters always stick together."

This was *definitely* some kind of futuristic shield-maiden group. But they were all so . . . bubbly. Maybe they didn't have hostile takeovers here?

"The chef serves breakfast, lunch, and dinner every day at the posted hours." Kayla pointed to a small sign on the counter. "All meals except Monday night dinner are casual dress, unless it's a costume night or we have an exchange with a fraternity. Then, of course, you dress to the theme."

"It sounds like you have many social events," Brigga said.

"So many," Meri said. "We have to give Lexi *some* reason to call us in for rebuke."

"Why would she do that?" I turned to study the girl whose strawberry-hued hair was several shades blonder—and considerably sleeker—than mine.

"Because." Lexi flicked a loose, frizz-free curl over her shoulder. "I'm the ethics chair. It's my job to make sure none of our sisters embarrass the sorority with their poor behavior."

These shieldmaidens had made the mean girl their enforcer? *Seems like a questionable life choice.*

"Oh, don't worry about us." Janna spoke up. "We're held to *extremely* high standards where we're from."

She wasn't wrong. Valkyris was the peak of virtue and honor—the pillar to which the rest of the Northern territories would one day be upheld. We hoped.

"Mmm." Lexi stared down her thin nose. "We'll see about that."

I bristled. "What's that supposed to mean?"

"Only that the reputation of this chapter is *very* important," Lexi said coolly. "And I won't have anyone tarnish it."

I stepped forward, but was stopped by Janna's firm hand on my chest.

"Like I said," Janna interjected. "We have *extremely* high standards. For ourselves, and for the people we associate with."

Lexi's nostrils flared. Before she could open her mouth, Kayla spoke up.

"Meri and I can take it from here." Kayla waved at Lexi and the rest of the girls who'd huddled around the foot of the staircase. A bevy of curious stares colored their smiling faces. "We'll have plenty of time to hang out with our new sisters at tonight's Halloween party. Right now, I'm sure they're exhausted from their travel day, and they just want to find their room and sleep."

"Thank you all for your hospitality." Janna folded her hands and bowed at the gaggle of girls. "We look forward to getting to know each and every one of you."

"At the . . . Halloween party," I added. What the Helheim was a Halloween?

"Go on." Kayla waved again, and the group dispersed. She and Meri led us up the switchback staircase, past the stained-glass window, and to the second floor. I adjusted my pack at the top of the stairs, shifting it against my shouldered shield before following Kayla around the square landing.

"Just a quick tour. Pledge porch is in there." She pointed to a room on her right. Inside stood twin rows of two-tiered beds. "Eight bunk beds house sixteen of our sophomores—they're not pledges, but we don't let freshmen live in-house, so . . ."

Bunk beds. They slept stacked on top of each other? We didn't have anything like this back home. Accommodations in the shieldmaiden compound were more spartan than in the castle, but even first-years had our own living quarters. Still, we were lucky—in my home village, each family's dwelling had been comprised of a single room. Back there, stacked beds—or beds at all—would have been a luxury.

"Over here are the officers' rooms. Meri and I share that one." Kayla pointed. Meri ducked inside, emerging a moment later with three folders tucked in her arms. "Lexi and Becky, our ethics chair and deputy ethics chair, are in there. And Devyn, our rush chair, shares with Ali, our treasurer. That hallway down there has five rooms off either side, each holding anywhere from two to six girls."

Wow. That meant . . . I ran a quick sequence in my head. "You have fifty girls living here?"

"Sixty-five, including you and our housemother." Meri smiled. "We have a few more rooms downstairs by the library."

"And all of you attend the academy down the road?" Brigga asked.

"All except our housemother," Meri clarified. "She's actually an alumnae of our rival school. But we don't hold it against her."

Right.

"There's an empty triple here in the officer's wing." Kayla gestured toward an open doorway. "I think you guys will like it. It's pretty big, so it has single beds instead of bunks. And it has a private bathroom, just like the rest of the officers' rooms. Check it out."

I nodded at Janna, who followed Kayla into what would be our quarters while we searched for the dark mage. Brigga stepped in ahead of me, and I trailed slightly behind her.

"Holy mother Frigga," Brigga blurted.

I lunged forward. My hand was already on my sword's hilt, ready to dispatch of the threat. But when I cleared the doorway, I found only tall windows, plush beds, and a trio of dressers inside a pentagon-shaped room. One wall housed another doorway, in which Brigga stood, gaping.

"This washroom is *amazing!*" Brigga's hands were over her mouth. "Ingrid, get in here. Look at how big their bucketless bath is!"

"Bucketless bath?" Meri laughed as she and Kayla

walked into the sleeping quarters. "Is that what you call them in Oslo?"

"Yes, in Oslo," I said quickly. "We have fun names for everything there. Why? What do you call them here?"

"We just call it a bathtub. One with jets, of course." Kayla shrugged. "All the officers' rooms have them. The other girls have communal bathrooms, down the hall."

So, this squadron had a class system? Apparently, the future hadn't progressed as far as we'd hoped.

"I'll leave welcome packets on your beds." Meri dropped a folder on each of the plush, white duvets. "House rules, dining and library schedules, internet password, and social calendar are all inside."

Internet password?

"We'll leave you to get settled. You really only brought a backpack each?" Kayla tilted her head.

"*Ja.*" Brigga backed slowly out of the washroom. "Do most of your guests bring more?"

"We don't have many guests here." Kayla laughed. "But personally, I've never traveled that light. Like, *ever.* If you forgot anything, just let Meri or I know. There's a drugstore down the street, and the closest mall's about twenty minutes away. I'm guessing you don't have a car yet, so we can drive you there."

Car. I shuddered at the memory of the angry man from the road. I wasn't sure I wanted to get into one of those metal carriages.

"Thank you. That's very kind." Janna bowed her

head to our hosts. "We'll just unpack our things, and join you for dinner at . . ."

She flipped open the folder on the bed, and scanned the top piece of parchment.

"At six," Meri offered. "We'll walk over to the Alpha's Halloween party a little after eight. Love your costumes, by the way."

"Totally." Kayla gestured to my leather pants, fitted tunic, and cloak. "Did you make that outfit yourself, or did you order it online?"

Was online what they called their seamstresses? Not wanting to guess wrong, I shrugged. "We, uh, made our outfits. Not our weapons, though. Those were made for us."

By the onlines?

"Wow! You guys should teach a costuming class for us! Vikings are big right now. Totally on trend." Kayla bounced on her toes.

"Vikings?" Brigga tilted her head.

Kayla paused. "You *do* still call yourselves Vikings, right? Is there another term in Norway? Oh, god. Is that not politically correct? I swear, everything changes so fast."

"No," I said, too quickly. "That's the word. Sorry, we're just, uh, tired."

And so very confused.

"Come on, Kayla." Meri laughed. "Let them get some rest. They're probably super jet-lagged."

"Fine." Kayla sighed. "See you guys in a bit. We're just across the landing if you need us."

"Thank you," Janna said. "We really appreciate everything."

Meri ushered Kayla outside, then closed the door behind her. When their voices had faded, I dropped onto the nearest bed and exhaled.

What exactly had we gotten ourselves into?

CHAPTER 5

I T ONLY TOOK A few minutes to transfer the contents of our packs into our dresser drawers. Unfortunately, we'd brought just two changes of clothes—each of which closely resembled what we were already wearing. We'd have to improvise if we didn't want our new squadron to think we wore 'Viking costumes' every day.

But that was tomorrow's problem. More pressing was our need to figure out how to blend into a dining room filled with girls whose daily reality was literally one thousand years from our own. Kayla had insisted that Janna, Brigga, and I sit at the officers' table. Now she, Meri, Devyn, and Ali were making us laugh with stories about their most recent fraternity exchange.

"Oh my god, you guys. That is *not* how last weekend's party ended!" Ali flipped her white-blond waves over one shoulder. "It *wasn't* a smoke alarm that made us evac—it was one of those air horns. The Zeta pledges brought it to the Alpha house as a rush prank. Earned them points with their big brothers."

"If it wasn't a smoke alarm, why did the firemen show up?" Devyn pressed a multipronged utensil into an herb-covered vegetable.

They don't knife everything here? Also, what is that amazing-smelling vegetable?

"The Zetas must have called nine-one-one." Ali shrugged. "Wouldn't be the first time they went to extreme measures to get our attention."

"Your sisterhood has many male admirers." Janna took a bite of chicken.

"We *are* the most selective sorority at SoCal State." Kayla sipped her water. "What about your chapter? If they all look like you, I'm sure the Oslo K. Mus have a social calendar that's *packed* with exchanges."

Exchanges were parties. We were exchange students. We lived in Oslo. We knew all about the pronged utensil and herb-covered vegetable.

I am so lost.

"Shoot!" Kayla frowned as her pronged utensil clattered to the floor. "I dropped my fork. I'll be right back."

She stood and crossed the room, retrieving another utensil from the counter. As she walked back, I committed its name to memory.

Fork. Fork. Fork. Fork.

"I looked over your social schedule," I said as I picked up my own fork and used it to lift one of the herbed vegetables. "You really have parties every weekend? How do you keep up with your studies?"

"We just do." Meri shrugged. "Our chapter prioritizes academics, so we have mandatory study hours—members are required to log fifteen hours weekly in either our sorority library, or one of the on-campus ones. We use the buddy system to enforce honesty, and lying about hours is a high-level ethics breach—automatic red card on exchanges for two weeks."

"Red card?" Brigga asked.

"No parties allowed." Devyn shook her head.

Right. I brought the vegetable to my mouth. A burst of flavor exploded across my tongue.

"My gods." I turned to Janna. "This is incredible."

She nodded, her mouth too full to do more than mutter, "Mm-hmm."

"It's our housemother's potato recipe," Ali said proudly. "Her grandmother perfected the rosemary seasoning. It was featured in *Southern Culinary Magazine*."

Potato. Potato. Potato. Potato.

Future-vegetables were *way* better than carrots.

"Will we need to log our study hours as well?" Brigga circled back. Smart. It would be easier to blend in, and thereby *not* get kicked out of our super-comfortable living arrangement, if we knew what was expected.

"You will," Meri confirmed. "And your volunteer hours, too. We're each supposed to put in a minimum of five hours a month for our charity—the women's shelter on Balboa Street. You can do stuff here, like prepping craft projects for the kids who live there, or if you'd rather be on-site, we have a monthly event there with the Alphas. They're our brother fraternity, so we do a lot with them."

"Plus Kayla's dating their president, so it makes things easier for her." Ali speared her salad.

"Multitasking for the win." Kayla smiled coyly.

"What else should we know that's not covered in the folder upstairs?" Brigga kept us on point.

"Curfew's fifteen minutes past midnight," Devyn offered. "Make sure you're back in the house by then, or it's an ethics write-up."

"Why fifteen minutes past?" Janna asked.

"We tried midnight and it didn't work," Ali confessed.

"Apparently, the girls here are incapable of being punctual." Kayla dabbed the corner of her mouth with her napkin.

"You're one to talk," Devyn countered. "You and Mike were the worst offenders."

Kayla raised her chin. "I have no idea what you're talking about."

Meri arched one brow. "Mm-hmm."

"Rude." Kayla stabbed a potato with her fork. "Our new sisters were asking how we balance our social and academic lives. The takeaway *should* be that we have the highest grade-point average on The Row. And the highest charitable score, too."

"The Row?" I asked.

"It's what we call the street with all the sororities and fraternities," Kayla explained. "What do you call yours?"

"Oh. Uh . . ." My eyes darted to Janna.

"The same," she said quickly. "Just in, you know, Norwegian."

"Right. Language barrier." Ali looked at me sympathetically. "You guys speak such good English. I wish I was bilingual."

The magical inner-ear translators definitely helped. *Thank you, Freia.*

"What classes are you taking this term?" Ali asked Janna.

Classes? Oh, gods. We were supposed to be enrolled in actual school. How were we going to fake that?

"Oh, the usual." Janna waved casually.

"General ed? Nice." Devyn finished off her chicken.

"Yes. It *is* nice," Janna said calmly. "Though we haven't seen our actual class schedule yet. Any idea where we might be able find it?"

"The school didn't e-mail it to you?" Meri frowned. "Did you check your phones? Maybe it's in spam."

"Well . . ." Janna blinked. I didn't blame her. The only words I'd understood in those sentences had been *school* and *the*.

"You *did* bring your phones from Norway, didn't you?" Meri reached into her pocket and pulled out one of the rectangular boxes everyone had been staring at on campus. "You just have to sync your plan with a

57

local server, and it should work just fine. That's what I did when I studied abroad last year."

"Oh, our *phones*." I nodded wisely. "No, we left them at home. Wanted a fresh start."

"You're off the grid?" Kayla's eyes widened. "That's *really* admirable. Good for you."

"Yeah. Way to be fully present." Devyn blinked. "That's like, next-level mindfulness."

"It is. Next level is definitely what we strive for." Brigga's stony face nearly made me laugh. Despite our translators, I'd never been more confused. But we were doing our best.

It was all we could do.

"You should come to our weekday morning yoga classes," Meri said. "Kayla's sister, Kenzi, leads them in the workout room next to the library. We don't get a lot of girls because, well, you know. Mornings."

"Mornings?" Brigga asked.

"Most of us don't have class until ten, so nobody's up at six—much less working out." Ali laughed. "But that's when Kenzi does it, and she refuses to change the time. Bless her heart."

I glanced at my captain. The Shieldmaiden Squadron went through a full workout before we sat for breakfast. Janna believed that hitting the ground running—literally—was the most efficient way to set our intentions for the day. Success waited for no woman.

"We'll come to Kenzi's class," Janna said. "Is it tomorrow?"

"She does it Monday through Friday, so yeah." Kayla glanced at her phone. "We'd better wrap dinner up. Lexi wants to go over some ethics guidelines in light of last week's, uh, behavior."

"What happened?" I hurriedly finished my *delicious* future vegetables.

"Two girls were dancing on tables at our last exchange." Meri's brows furrowed. "It reflected poorly on the chapter as a whole."

"You know they got pulled up there." Devyn shook her head. "Tiffani jumped down as soon as Pete let her go."

"Yeah, but Tara didn't. And she created *quite* the scene," Meri said.

A gentle chime filled the air as Kayla pressed a pink fingernail to her phone. The conversations around us immediately ceased as Kayla put her napkin on the table, and stood.

"Evening, ladies." Kayla raised one hand in a wave.

The fifty girls in the room each chirped a cheery response.

"I'm sure you're all ready to party—or, you will be after you put on your costumes." Kayla grinned. "Lexi's going to go over a few ground rules before we dismiss for prep-time, but first I'd like to officially introduce our newest sisters—Janna, Ingrid, and Brigga, from the Oslo chapter of Kappa Mu. They're brand-new here. They haven't even seen their class schedule yet, poor things! Morgan, are you still doing your work study at the registrar's office? Think you can help them out?"

"Of course." A chipper redhead with a cropped pixie cut beamed from the back of the room. "I can look up your classes after dinner—I'll just pop by your room when we're all done eating."

"Oh, that's really not necessary." I smiled, hoping a grin would hide the fact that blood was rapidly draining from my face. "We'll figure it out and—"

"No worries. I'm happy to help." Morgan dismissed my objection with a wave of her hand.

Well, then.

"Now that that's settled, Lexi?" Kayla held out her arm. "The floor is yours."

Lexi waltzed to the front of the dining room. Her too-short skirt swayed as she jutted her hip and launched into a lecture about decorum, and standards, and not embarrassing the sanctity of 'K. Mu.' Which seemed ironic, given that her outfit was so miniscule. Was this how most girls dressed here? Or was it just the mean ones?

When Lexi finished, Kayla dismissed us all to go upstairs and change into our costumes. "Except for you three. You're already perfect Vikings! You have to tell us how you made those outfits. They're so authentic."

"What they have to do is figure out what class they're supposed to go to in the morning." Morgan waved us up the stairs. "You're in the three-person off the officers' landing, right? I'll grab my laptop and meet you there. We'll figure this out together."

"Great," Brigga croaked.

Janna, Brigga, and I hung a left at the top of the

stairs. Once we reached our room, I headed straight for my bed, flopped down on the duvet, and sighed. "What now?"

"Now we find your classes." Morgan's cheerful voice came from the doorway. I sat up with a jolt, sliding until my back was nestled against the headboard. How was she that fast?

"Um. Thank you, Morgan," Janna said tactfully. "But we're more than capable of finding our—"

"I told you, no worries." Morgan sat on the edge of my bed and opened a rectangular device. It lit up with a *ping*, revealing an image of Morgan surrounded by girls, each wearing a 'Kappa Mu' T-shirt. "That's my pledge class—we took this at last year's carnival for the shelter," she said with a smile. "We put on a big event every fall for the kids. It's really fun."

"I'll bet." I leaned closer. Each of the girls wore a huge smile. It was clear they valued their friendships.

"Now, we had three transfer students from Oslo scheduled to join the sophomore class." Morgan pressed a series of buttons, and the image shifted to a list of names. "I remember because I'm in charge of processing transfer schedules and credits for this term. I just do the data entry, which I usually zone out on. But I remembered you guys because Kayla said our house was getting transfers from Oslo, too. Later, I was told that you changed your minds, so I never finished processing your classes. But . . . huh."

"Huh what?" Brigga peered over Morgan's shoulder.

"That's weird. The Oslo transfers have different

names. I wonder if there was a mixup, or . . ." Morgan squinted at the screen.

I bit nervously on my bottom lip. Of course they did. *Because we weren't them!*

"We go by our middle names," Janna said calmly. "It's customary where we're from."

I held my breath. But Morgan shrugged, seeming to accept the explanation without issue.

"That makes sense. Looks like we had you down for . . ." Morgan pressed an arrow and the image rolled down. "Ah, there you go. It was folklore, astronomy, and rocks for jocks."

"Excuse me?" Brigga's eyebrows rose.

"Geology." Morgan laughed. "It's super easy, so most of the football players take it."

"Ah," I said wisely. Because I *absolutely* knew what football was.

"I'll just finish filling out your enrollment, and . . . done." Morgan closed her laptop. "You're set again. Sorry about the confusion—I really don't know what happened."

"Well, we're here now." I shrugged. "So, uh, thank you?"

"Of course!" Morgan stood up and walked toward the door. "I'll print the schedules out in my room, and leave them on your beds, along with a map. I'm in your folklore class, so I can walk you over tomorrow morning. Want to meet downstairs at ten?"

"Sounds like a plan. Thanks again." I smiled.

"Yeah, thanks, Morgan." Janna raised one hand. "We'll see you in the morning."

"You'll see me sooner than that." Morgan laughed. "We always walk over to exchanges as a house. I'd better get changed—you three are *definitely* winning the costume contest this year. Way to play to your theme."

With that, Morgan turned and darted across the landing. When she'd gone from view, I stood, crossed the room, and closed our door. Then I turned to Janna and Brigga with a bewildered stare.

How were we going to fake our way through this one?

An hour later, I found myself at my first ever 'frat party'—a term I was pretty sure was future-code for 'mead-fest.' I'd come here to track a dark mage on my first ever shieldmaiden mission. Instead, I was searching for Axel and Raynor in a sea of inebriated, handsy men.

Blech.

I'd lost count of the number of passes I'd refused since I'd arrived at the Alpha house. Unlike Valkyris' rigidly structured, tradition-filled balls, this 'exchange' seemed to be a drunken free-for-all. The backyard of our neighboring castle was covered in a wooden dance floor, on which a multitude of my new 'sisters' writhed against a sea of muscled males. This so-called 'dancing' was likely to score an ethics interrogation from the steely eyed Lexi, though she seemed to be shooting more cold glares in my direction than at her more scantily clad subjects. The remainder of the girls stood casually around the pool, where a handful of shirtless guys floated on round tubes. Mead flowed freely from a metal canister, and food-lined tables stood at the far edge of the yard. This event was unlike anything we'd seen back home. But at least nobody was commenting on our outfits . . . or the weapons we'd strapped on before we'd left our room. Besides my shield and sword, I had the tracking vial in my pouch, and our time-traveling dagger concealed in its sheath at my waist. I was ready to bring in the dark mage.

Just as soon as I found him.

"I see Axel." Janna squinted against the glare of flashing lights. "He and Raynor are on the other side of the dance floor."

I followed her sight line, and was promptly filled with a surge of irritation. "Better get to them fast. Looks like Lexi and Becky are on the move."

Brigga jutted her hip as the girls strutted toward our teammates. "I don't trust those two."

"Neither do I. Come on." I grabbed Brigga's hand and dragged her down the porch steps and across the yard. When we reached our colleagues, they were already deep in conversation with the ethics chair and her deputy. I bit on my bottom lip and struggled to swallow my distaste. Both of the girls wore variations on the tight sweaters and miniscule skirts they'd donned that afternoon—all white ensembles with a red cross atop their chests, and little white hats on their heads.

The future was a seriously weird place.

Becky reached up to stroke Raynor's arm, and Brigga's hand tightened around mine. I didn't know if she had a thing with the Halvarssons' sometimes-surly son, but she definitely had a history with Axel. It was ironic that she was annoyed with another girl for playing what we all knew was *her* game. I, of course, was annoyed for a different reason. We were on a mission, and *all* of my team needed to be on top of their game.

Including the stupid males currently ogling my *sisters'* chests.

Men.

"Raynor." Brigga elbowed past Becky. "I need to talk to you."

"Raynor was talking to *me*." Becky batted her unnaturally long lashes. "Weren't you, Raynor?"

Raynor's eyes darted between Becky's breasts and Brigga's glare.

"I was," he said cautiously. "But, uh . . ."

"*Now.*" Brigga grabbed Raynor's wrist and dragged him away from the brunette.

"Yeah. Come on. We need to go." I ignored the surge of annoyance that churned in my gut. Lexi had her chest pressed against Axel's bicep—an intimacy no self-respecting Valkyris woman would ever presume with a man who was, again, *not her husband*. What had happened to propriety—or even modesty—in the past thousand years? Or the next thousand years? I struggled to wrap my head around where—and when—I was. Was this the jet lag Meri had mentioned?

"Leaving so soon, Axel?" Lexi stuck out her bottom lip. "We were only just getting to know each other."

"There's plenty of time for that. Hold my drink?" Axel winked at Lexi. She shot me a triumphant grin as she accepted her prize.

"Hurry back," Lexi said breathily.

Double blech.

I wrapped my hand around Axel's considerable bicep, and dragged him away from the village trollop.

"Gods, Ingrid. In a hurry?" Axel shrugged out of my grasp, and rubbed his arm. No doubt it hurt from where my fingernails had dug into his flesh. *On purpose.*

"Yes, I'm in a hurry. And you should be too." I stopped when I reached Raynor and Brigga. "There's a dark mage on the loose, and his trail's getting colder by the minute. I'd think completing Freia's mission would be more important to you than . . ." I waved at the sea of writhers. ". . . whatever you're doing with *her*."

"Why, Ingrid Tirsdatter." Axel grinned. "Are you jealous?"

"What? No," I dismissed him. "I just don't appreciate working with a teammate who doesn't prioritize the mission."

"Who says I can't do more than one thing? I can be very efficient." Axel leaned close to whisper into my ear. "Or I can be *very* meticulous. Depending on the situation."

66

Oh. My. Gods.

Heat built along my cheeks, and I quickly pushed it down. Axel was beyond arrogant. If we weren't in public, I'd use my shield to pop him right in his perfectly square, neatly trimmed jawline.

"There you are—I lost you in this crowd." Janna's low voice pulled my focus. "We have to leave. We need to make a plan, and Ingrid's attracting too much attention."

"No. I'm blending just as well as you are." I gestured to my captain and our disseminator.

"If that's the case, why have you been asked to dance twice as often as we have? Combined?" Janna pointed to my hair, which I'd wrangled into wild, loose curls. "Maybe the men of the future are into redheads."

Brigga arched her brow and pointed to my chest. "More likely they're into *those*."

Axel's smirk deepened. "I'm sure they are."

I growled as I slugged him in the stomach. His muscles were so hard, it probably hurt me more than it did him.

Stupid assassin.

"What?" He shrugged. "Future men aren't blind."

The heat returned to my cheeks, and I hurriedly crossed my arms over my chest. I'd opted to wear my training tunic tonight. Its low neckline and sleeveless design made it easier to fight in, Odin willing the evening brought us into contact with the dark mage. But I hadn't counted on the attention my cleavage would receive from the manner-averse Alphas.

Or from the now-staring Axel.

"Don't you have a job to do?" I hissed.

"Like I said." Axel's dimple popped. "I'm efficient."

So help me, gods, I will *kill him before this mission's over.*

I squared my shoulders, turned to Janna, and awaited my instructions.

Soon, my team stood huddled inside a classroom at Southern California State. The string of castles on our road were each filled with raucous music, inebriated students, and what seemed to be an endless stream of lawn-top dance floors. It was hardly the environment in which to brief a team, so Janna had steered us back toward the relative quiet of the students' academy. Unlike ours back home, this one was mostly deserted at nighttime. Bizarre as this seemed, it gave us enough cover to discuss our plan.

Or, more accurately, our lack of one.

"We have no idea where the target is." Raynor dropped onto one of the desks that lined the classroom. "None."

"The dagger brought us to the last-known location of his whereabouts," Janna reiterated. "Which means at some point today, he was here—on this campus."

"Unless he wasn't." Brigga glanced up from the piece of parchment on which she scribbled her notes.

"Freia told us we'd be coming to a coastal town. I don't see the ocean anywhere. Maybe we missed our mark."

"Los Angeles *is* a coastal town. Look at this." Axel spoke from the back of the classroom. He was studying some kind of a map. It looked different from the ones we used back home—this one was divided up into squares, and filled in with colors and strange lines.

I pushed away from the window, and followed Janna and Brigga to the back of the room.

"Raynor, get up." I deliberately bumped his elbow as I walked by.

"A map doesn't help us," Raynor complained. "Unless it's got a glowing star that says *YOUR TARGET IS HERE.*"

"Well, it doesn't *not* help us," I said over my shoulder. "Get off your butt and make yourself useful."

"Somebody's in a mood," Raynor griped. But he followed me to the back of the room. "Fine, Andersson. Show us the coastal town of *Los Angeles.*"

"The village is bordered by ocean to the west. Look." Axel pointed to the map. Sure enough, Los Angeles was marked as a dot roughly half an inch inland from the Pacific Ocean. If the key at its bottom was correct, it appeared we were currently a good distance from the *actual* oceanfront towns of Santa Monica, Manhattan Beach, and Hermosa Beach.

"So, maybe the target is in one of those places?" Raynor jabbed his finger at the map.

"Maybe," Axel said doubtfully. "But Freia was pretty

convinced the dagger would take us to his *actual* location."

"Ten miles off isn't terrible," I conceded. "In the scope of five thousand."

"You think we need to go west, then?" Brigga stared at the map. "How do we choose which village to search?"

"And how do we get there?" Janna frowned. "We don't have horses, or dragons, or even one of those metal carts."

"Cars," I reminded her. "They're called cars."

"Right." Janna rested her hand on the hilt of her sword. "But even if we did have a . . . car, we wouldn't know how to operate it."

"I'm pretty sure I could figure it out." Axel grinned over his shoulder. "Can't be harder than flying a dragon."

"Well, it's a non-issue because we aren't currently in possession of one." Janna turned to me. "Ingrid, you're our tracker. What's your instinct say?"

"We've only got one shot with the trace, so I don't want to use it until we're sure we're within range of the target." I reached behind my back to run my fingers over my shield. "The dagger dropped us just outside this building, so he must have been here recently."

"Maybe he moved to one of these other villages . . ." Raynor squinted at the map. "Her-moose-uh Beach, or Santa Moh-nee-kuh."

"Maybe." I shrugged. "But we're here, not there. So my recommendation is to go outside, and scour the grounds for any evidence of our target. Valkyris uses *älva* dust to power our magic, which leaves behind a sheer, golden film. I'm not sure what dark mages use, but if his magic carries any residue, and if he's used it in the vicinity, we should be able to find something."

Brigga glanced down at her parchment. "Disseminators study mages in our final semester. We're taught that those who channel dark energies tap into a negative frequency—one that emits a cloud of darkness."

"Like smoke?" Janna asked.

"Kind of." Brigga tugged on her braid. "I remember seeing it with my sister's reanimated dragon . . . after she turned on us and fought for Bjorn."

"That was *your* dragon," I whispered to Axel.

"The dragon *you* made me leave behind," he lobbed.

"Like we had any other choice! Clan Bjorn would have captured us if we'd stayed around another minute —no telling what they'd have had time to do if we tried to drag your dead dragon onto that tiny escape boat and—"

"Ingrid. Axel. That's enough." Janna's reprimand made me jump. "Brigga, what does a dark mage's residue look like?"

"With my sister's dragon—"

Axel shot me a sideways look. I glared back at him.

"It was sort of a mist," Brigga continued. "A faint, dirty smoke that rose off the creature's back. Like when we burn old wood."

"That's how I remember it, too," Axel confirmed. "It

also had a sheen, as if light was refracting off its particles."

I shot the assassin a look. "I was unaware you were familiar with refraction."

"I'm familiar with a lot of things." Axel shrugged. "I *am* more than just a gorgeous face, you know."

I rolled my eyes as I turned back to Brigga. "With that information, we'll search for a residue that resembles dirty smoke. Spread out, and signal the group if you come across something. I've got a kit in my pouch that can help with any airborne samples, so I'll test the air while the rest of you search the grounds. If we haven't turned anything up in thirty minutes, we'll expand our parameters . . . and consider sending small breakout units to the beach cities."

"I claim Santa Moh-nee-kuh," Raynor spoke up.

"Why?" I asked.

"It looks like fun." Raynor picked up a booklet from the table below the map. *Santa Monica Review* was printed on its cover, along with the image of a round, illuminated wheel atop a boarded walkway. Raynor pointed to the wheel. "I'm sure this aerial viewing device would make an excellent watchtower."

"Fine. If this search fails, you can captain the Santa Monica search unit. But right now, I want everyone outside." I waved my team toward the door. "We've got a target to track."

CHAPTER 6

TWENTY MINUTES LATER, OUR search had turned up nothing more than a handful of trash, and a smattering of dried-out leaves. My tests had revealed the air quality of Los Angeles was below abysmal—either the dark mage had visited literally ever corner of campus, or the air of the future was so bad that it triggered alarm-levels in my test kit. I'd never seen readings this poor back home—not even after the siege on Valkyris.

And the villagers actually breathed this stuff?

"I'm calling it. This search was a bust," I said when I returned to the park. "Nothing's out of the ordinary— or everything's out of the ordinary. I'm not sure which."

"We didn't find anything, either," Janna said as she and Axel headed my way.

"Same here," Brigga called. She and Raynor approached from behind a building. "We went to the western end of campus. We figured maybe if he'd gone toward the beaches, he'd have left a trail. But either he's really good at cleaning up after himself, or—"

BOOM!

The clap of thunder pulled my attention upward. I spun in a quick rotation, noting the inky-blue sky, faint smattering of stars . . . and complete absence of clouds.

I immediately unshouldered my shield. "Anybody see the source of that noise?"

"Negative." Axel drew his broadsword. "But it definitely didn't come from the sky."

"Or maybe it did." Janna pointed with her own weapon. Its silver blade angled toward a dim light I hadn't noticed before. Its source must have been somewhere behind the nearest structure—its faint glow illuminated the brick tower as if it were a halo.

"Is it a fire?" Raynor guessed. "I smell smoke."

"I do too. But it's different, somehow." The pungent tang of sulfur filled my head, and a memory needled at the back of my brain. The only other time I'd inhaled that twisted scent, Brigga's sister, Birna, had stood raging beside her still-smoking dragon. She'd hurtled insults at us, all the while blaming everyone but herself for the nightmare she'd found herself in. It was the last time I'd seen her alive. And if this smoke came from the same source, it could only mean one thing.

Dark magic was nearby.

Game on.

I squared my shoulders toward the source. "Axel, do

74

you remember the stench coming off Birna's dragon? Doesn't this remind you of—"

"It's definitely a match." Axel raised his sword to the building. "Raynor, get Brigga out of here. The target's in the vicinity."

"I'm not helpless," Brigga objected. But as she pulled a dagger from her waist, she stepped slightly behind Raynor.

"Stay there," Raynor cautioned. "Janna, what's the strategy on—Janna?"

My captain had already taken off at a sprint. Axel and I followed quickly behind her. We rounded the ivy-lined corner of the building just as Janna disappeared from view.

Axel swore. "Where'd she g—"

A piercing shriek filled the air. I whirled around. Raynor was immobilized behind me. He'd lunged forward in almost a defensive position, his body blocking Brigga from an unseen assault. The blonde stood frozen with her hands over her mouth, eyes wide in fear as she stared at a glimmering, black mist that encased both her and Raynor.

"Brigga, run!" I shouted. But she remained immobile, still as the sword-wielding statue of a Spartan positioned behind her in the quad. Double *dritt.* "Axel, it's the smoke—the target's got Brigga and Raynor in some kind of hold. We have to—oh, gods!"

My stomach clenched as I stumbled upon my teammate surrounded by darkness and frozen in a half-leap. Axel's body was angled toward me, as if he'd tried to intercept the mist for the both of us. Considering I was still mobile and he was completely frozen, he must have succeeded. Which meant . . .

"Janna!" I screamed. I covered my nose as I ran around the mist, unsure whether contact or inhalation rendered its victims helpless. "Don't breathe or touch the—"

"It's too late. They've all been incapacitated." A gravelly voice echoed off the buildings. It was low, menacing, and it bore the edge of someone who'd come slightly unhinged.

Where is he?

I shifted my shield in front of my body, and sprinted toward the nearest cover. The Spartan statue wasn't wide, but I hoped it was dense enough to deflect —or at least slow down—another mist attack. I charged across the quad, racing toward the obstruction.

Once I'd reached the sculpture, I pressed my back to its base and crooked my arm so that my shield obscured my face. Panic seized my gut, the reality of what I was up against rocking me to my core. My entire team had been disabled . . . and I wasn't sure where the next assault would come from.

Breathe, Ingrid. No, don't breathe. Dark magic mist is toxic. I think. Just . . . don't get frozen.

I adjusted my grip on my sword and waited.

"It's no fun if you're not going to play." The voice was unnervingly close. I swung around the statue, careful to keep its brick base between me and my attacker. A thick, black mist whooshed through the air, and I held my breath. I dropped lower, folding myself into a ball and pressing tight against the spot where the statue met the ground.

As the darkness moved around me, I pulled my arm into my chest. My shield formed an imperfect barrier between the mist and me, but it must have been enough. I counted to ten, careful not to inhale while the darkness swirled through the air. Then I peeked around the edge of my shield and waited for the mist to creep away. It slithered like a serpent, eking its black trail across the ground before evaporating like water off the hot springs back home.

Now what?

"Are you hiding?" The voice chuckled. "You clever, little thing. I always did enjoy a good hunt."

CRACK!

The ground trembled, and the bricks at my back shifted sharply. I tilted my shield just as the statue splintered overhead. Its head dropped abruptly, landing with a *clang* mere inches from my feet. As soon as it hit, its remains wobbled atop their unstable base. If I didn't move soon, I'd be crushed by a headless, iron Spartan. But if I gave up my cover, I'd be fully exposed. I only had a second to—

BOOM!

I ducked beneath my shield as what was left of the statue burst into shards. They rained down on my cover, pelting its surface with heavy thuds. My arm strained against the battery, but the moment it ended

I'd have a decision to make: face a dark mage alone, or run. Only one of those options offered any chance of survival.

But I'd never been a coward.

"Argh!" I ripped my shield from my face and leapt to my feet. My sword barely trembled as I charged around the remains of the statue. The dark mage stood fifty feet away. I didn't break my stride as I set him in my sights, cataloguing his weaknesses as I ran. He was short, standing substantially smaller than my five-feet, seven-inches. And he was out of shape, given the doughiness of his jowls and the breadth of fabric that made up his cloak. But he was formidable enough to raise both arms and crook his fingers to his palms. Darkness pulsed between his hands, and I threw myself to the side just as he launched another assault.

My shoulder collided with the ground as I rolled out of the mist's path, grateful for the training that had taught me how to anticipate attacks. I quickly leapt to my feet, keeping my shield in front of me as I lifted my shoulder and set my course. Twenty more feet and my sword would strike. My breath came in ragged gasps as I pumped my legs harder. Fifteen feet. *Ten. Five.*

The mage's lips pulled back and I lunged forward. In the second before I stabbed his heart, his eyes roved over my body. He was . . . searching for something. Something he must have known I had. There was no other reason for him to attack our group. *Was there?*

CLANG!

My sword struck soundly, the vibration of metal on

metal ringing throughout the air. My elbow shrieked in agony as the impact ricocheted up my arm. Though my aim had been true, the target I'd hit hadn't been the one I intended. My sword bounced firmly off of what was left of the Spartan. The statue had swapped spots with the dark mage, who now stood . . . I whipped my head around until I spotted him at the far end of the quad. He whirled one hand in a dramatic circle, sending black sparks spinning in an orb. When he lifted the other hand, the sparks converged to form a massive, round portal. The mage stepped inside of it, glancing over his shoulder as he moved. Just before the circle closed around him, his eyes met mine in a rage-filled glare. A half-second later, they dropped to my waist, pausing at the spot where Freia's dagger hung in its sheath. The mage's eyes lit up, and a small smile quirked at one lip as he was sucked into the darkness.

Oh. My. Gods.

As soon as he'd gone, a *whoosh* filled the air. The portal sucked in on itself, disappearing in a small vortex like water down a drain. Four thuds echoed from around the quad. I dropped to a fighting stance, preparing for the next attack. But a quick scan of the area revealed no new threats. The sound had come from my teammates. The thuds were their bodies cracking against the ground. They rubbed varied limbs as they scrambled to right themselves.

"Where'd Janna go?" Axel shouted. We'd been looking for her before he'd been immobilized, and the thought must have stayed fresh on his mind. He picked a stone from his beard and pushed himself to his feet as he muttered, "What the Helheim? Why am I on the ground?"

"We all are," Raynor said. "Brigga, are you all right?"

"I've been better," she groaned. She slid her feet in front of her so she sat on her backside. "What happened?"

"You got mage'd," I called out.

"Huh?" Three heads turned to look at me.

"Ingrid! You were just . . ." Axel glanced to his right. "Uh . . ."

"I was next to you," I confirmed. "You're not crazy. Well, no more than usual."

Axel shot me a look.

"Oh, thank gods you're all right." I exhaled at the sight of my captain as she made her way around the corner of a building.

"I am," Janna said. "But I'm very confused. I don't remember hitting the ground."

"The mage dusted everyone while we were chasing you down." I moved toward the center of the quad. "Way to get a jump on the rest of us."

Janna frowned. "I take it he escaped."

"He did," I confirmed. "He got you, then Axel, and Raynor and Brigga. I'm not sure how I avoided the first blow, but I evaded the rest by hiding behind that."

I pointed to what was left of the statue. Its once regal form had been reduced to smoking rubble.

Axel winced. "We'd better clear out before we're associated with the demolition."

"Good plan." Raynor helped Brigga to her feet. They walked toward me, and it didn't escape me that he held on to her hand for a few seconds longer than absolutely necessary.

Interesting.

"You managed to evade the mage? Well done, Ingrid." Janna clasped my arm.

"Thanks. But as you noticed, I didn't do much more than stay alive." I shook my head. "He opened a portal and got away."

"Thank gods he didn't take you with him," Axel said gruffly.

My pulse quickened. Did Axel actually care?

Stop it, Ingrid. It's not like that.

Obviously.

"Wait, he can *open portals?*" Brigga's lips formed a pert *O*. "Like, to other realms? Is he in another realm right now?"

"I don't know where he went," I said. "He could have gone back to where he's staying, or returned to wherever his powers come from, or even jumped years —he may be in Valkyris for all we know. He just walked through the portal and it sealed up behind him."

A fresh wave of frustration coursed through me. I'd been *this close* to a kill—to completing our mission and returning victorious to my chieftess. Instead, I was right back at square one—mage-less, lead-less, and pretty much hopeless.

What the Helheim were we supposed to do now?

"Hey." Axel's fingertips brushed my bare shoulder. A pulse of heat shot across my skin. "You okay?"

"No. I'm not." I jerked my arm away and folded it across my chest. "I lost our target."

Axel frowned as I stepped back. "Yeah, well. You're the only one of us who didn't get knocked out. So that's a win."

"I guess." I walked toward the spot where the portal had stood, in part to look for evidence and in part to get some space from the assassin whose scrutiny was unnerving. Ignoring Axel, I knelt on the stones and ran my fingertips across the rough ground. "Huh."

"What?" Janna moved to my side.

I raised two fingers to my face and squinted at the faint, grey residue. "We were looking for the wrong thing. This isn't soot—it's a . . . gaseous liquid? Is that even possible?"

"Not that I know of." Janna swiped her own fingers across the film. "It's oily . . . wait. It's gone."

"*Ja.* It stayed on my fingers for a few seconds, then it evaporated." I frowned. "But there's still a pretty substantial pool of it on the ground. There must be some kind of a reaction with my skin, or maybe my body heat, that changes it to a gas."

Janna frowned. "How do we retrieve a sample without touching it?"

"We don't," Axel said drily. "Ingrid, what's in your collection kit? Got anything that can get some of that evidence into a vial without contact?"

I rifled through the pouch that hung from my hip,

laying its contents on the ground beside me. "An eyedropper might work. Unless it's my body heat that activates the shift. If that's the case, I'll need a barrier." I withdrew the dropper and lowered it to the puddle of residue. Squeezing the ball at the end, I slowly pulled the liquid upward. The moment it pooled in the bulb, it shimmered and disappeared.

Shoot.

"Body heat activates the change of state," I confirmed. I slipped my hand beneath the hem of my top, and held the bulb through its fabric. This time when I drew up the liquid, it collected easily in the bulb . . . and stayed there. "Got it. Now I just need a—"

"Here." Axel picked up a vial, and held it steady. I transferred the contents of the dropper into the glass, careful to keep my fingers wrapped in fabric. Once the eyedropper was empty, I grabbed a stopper and plugged the tube.

"Don't touch the base," I warned.

"I have an idea." Axel passed me the sample, and I gingerly gripped it at its top while he removed one of the leather cuffs from his wrist. He wrapped it around the glass, then handed it back to me. "That should work."

"Thanks." I carefully placed the sample in my pouch before retrieving the rest of my kit. "I can test this back in my room—figure out what elements it carries. Though I don't know where we'd find them around here."

"It doesn't matter. Every bit of information helps," Janna said.

"It does," Axel confirmed. "And now we know what to look for."

"*Ja*. A disappearing liquid-gas." Raynor frowned.

"That's more than we had an hour ago." Janna pointed out.

Raynor merely grunted.

"So, now what do we do?" Brigga looked up from an ink-filled piece of parchment.

"Have you been taking notes?" I asked.

"I *am* a disseminator." She tossed her braid over her shoulder. "And if, Odin forbid, something happens to us, Freia would want a log of what we've learned."

I apprised my onetime nemesis. Maybe she was smarter than I'd thought.

"We need to study the sample." Janna glanced at my pouch. "And we'll need to do some research. Why did the mage come here? And now? What's unique in this time and location that he couldn't get/see/do/whatever back home?"

"And why did he target us tonight?" Axel asked. "We searched for half an hour and couldn't find so much as a trace of him. Why would he possibly give up his location and reveal himself?"

"I think I know." I palmed the hilt of Freia's dagger, still hanging snugly from my belt. "Right before the mage portaled out of here, he looked at this blade. I think he wants it."

"Freia's dagger?" Brigga's eyes widened. "Why

would he need her magic? He's a mage—he has his own."

"*Ja.*" Axel stroked his beard. "But maybe he doesn't want *us* to have any."

"You think he's jealous?" Brigga arched one brow.

"We're a threat," Axel said slowly. "We're obviously Valkyris—no other tribes have magic. He has to know we're here to end him."

"And now he knows what we look like, and where we are . . ." Janna sighed. "Maybe we should relocate."

"No." I shook my head. "We have a solid base. We've got more resources back at our temporary residences than we would if we struck out on our own. We have food, and shelter, and access to libraries, and, most importantly, an entire house filled with girls—or guys —who can help us figure out how to blend in so we're harder to identify."

Brigga narrowed her eyes. "What are you saying?"

"I'm saying I think we should stay put. Pretend we're students here, just like everyone thinks we are, and use this academy's resources to help us track the mage. He'll expect us to move out now that we've made contact. Why should we play into his hand?"

Janna nodded. "I like it. And not only because I *really* enjoyed those potatoes we had at dinner. Why don't we have potatoes in Valkyris?"

"Maybe they haven't been invented yet?" I offered.

"I like our room. And that bathtub," Brigga added sheepishly. "I wouldn't mind staying put while we gather more information."

"We've got a decent setup at our place," Axel agreed. "Did you know people here watch their sports inside a flat box attached to the wall? They don't even have to go outside."

"And they have a sauce-covered flatbread they load up with meat and cheese." Raynor spoke with a reverence. "We need to bring that thing home."

"So it's settled." I studied at my team. "We'll maintain our current base while we gather more information. And once we have another lead on the target . . ."

"We move out and strike." Axel crossed his arms. His biceps bulged with the movement.

They're just arms, Ingrid.

Big ones.

Ja . . .

I pulled my gaze away from Axel and focused on Janna. Her eyes darted between me and the assassin, and one corner of her mouth pulled up in a half-smile.

Oh, gods.

Heat crept up my neck. There was absolutely *no chance* of anything *ever* going on with me and Axel. He was arrogant, and insufferable, and irritating. Not to mention he'd been involved with at least half the female members of our tribe—including both Brigga and her sister. *Blech.*

I turned at the gong of the nearby clock tower. "What time is it?"

Axel craned his neck. "Midnight, I think. Why?"

"Curfew's in fifteen minutes," I said. "If we're planning to stick around, we'd better get back before Lexi pulls us in on an ethics violation."

Axel's eyes crinkled at the corners. "You girls have a curfew?"

Janna stepped onto the lamp-lit path that led back to our temporary residences. "You *don't* have a curfew?"

"Nope." Axel followed her with a shrug. "Plus we have pizza."

"What's pizza?" Brigga whispered.

"The flatbread I was talking about." Raynor raised his forearm, and Brigga looped her hand around it. "I'll bring some over tomorrow."

"What about you, shieldmaiden?" Axel arched his brow as I fell in step beside him. "You want pizza?"

"What I want is to catch the mage. This is my first mission, and I'm not going to let Freia and Halvar down." I ignored Axel's offered arm. And I *doubly* ignored the way he looked at me in the lamplight—with an intensity that almost bordered on longing.

What's going on with him?

"We'll catch our target." Axel didn't take his eyes off of me. "Your first assignment will be a win—I'll make sure of it."

"*You'll* make sure? Ugh." I quickened my pace. Leave it to Axel to turn a group effort into a one-man ego fest.

"Yes. I will." Axel matched my stride. "Not only is it my job, but I understand this means a great deal to you."

"*Ja*, Axel." I breezed past Raynor and Brigga. "The

security of Valkyris, not to mention the future of the world, *does* mean a great deal to me. Thanks for noticing."

Axel's fingers hooked my elbow. "Why are you mad?"

"I'm not mad." I wrenched my arm free. "I'm focused."

"Focused looks mad on you," Axel called as I stormed toward Janna. But I ignored him. I had a curfew to make, a 'sisterhood' to appease, and a dark mage to track.

And I had no idea how I was going to do any of it.

CHAPTER 7

MORNING CAME MUCH FASTER than I'd hoped. Fog filled my head as I rolled it off my pillow. Immediately, I was struck by the rhythm of an incessant pounding. Was the shieldmaiden compound under attack?

Oh, gods. Has Clan Bjorn come back for seconds?

My right arm flung instinctively to the hook by my bed, where I always hung my blade. But instead of a sword, my hand landed on something simultaneously firm and fluffy. I dragged my eyelids open and blinked at the feather-lined lampshade that was most definitely *not* in my quarters in the compound. Below it rested a small box that flashed the hour—05:45. And beyond that was a window through which muted sunlight streamed. It was time for my morning workout. But this was no shieldmaiden compound.

Where the Helheim was I?

"Janna? Ingrid? Brigga? It's Kenzi. Are you coming

89

to yoga?" The pounding echoed from my left. I whipped my head toward a door, eyeing my teammates' sleeping forms along the way. As I registered Janna and Brigga, and the plethora of baby blue filling my normally green-hued bedroom, everything came rushing back.

I was in a sorority house.

I was one thousand years in the future.

I'd agreed to attend something called *yoga*.

It was going to be a long day.

"Girls? Are you coming? I know it was a late night with the party and all, so if it's not your thing I totally understand." Kenzi's cheerful voice pierced the early morning quiet as I swung my legs off the bed and shuffled toward the closed door. "Just wanted to tell you that you're always welcome, and I'm more than happy to—oh. Hey!"

"Hey." I tried not to yawn over the word. "You must be the morning trainer."

"Trainer?" Kenzi tilted her head. With her big, doe eyes and glossy, black hair, she was easily recognizable as Kayla's sister. I poked my head out of my room. The sorority president's door was firmly shut. Morning enthusiasm must not have run in their family.

"You supervise the morning training sessions, *ja*?"

"Um, I lead our yoga classes, if that's what you mean. But I'm not a personal trainer or anything. I'm way too chill for that. I just do it for fun." Kenzi untied the silky ribbon at the bottom of her sweater, and I tried not to stare at what must have been her workout attire—tight, black leggings and a tiny scrap of black fabric that stretched across her chest like a tube.

None of my clothes looked like that.

"Um, Kenzi?" I leaned toward the not-a-trainer. "My friends and I packed pretty light. We forgot to bring our, uh . . ."

Kenzi watched me curiously as I stared at her clothes. "You guys don't have any workout gear? Oh, no worries. We have a *ton* in our castoff closet. That's where we put everything we want to give away. Any one of our sisters can pull anything she finds in there and keep it."

Relief coursed through me. "Perfect. Where is this closet?"

"Just behind the pledge porch." Kenzi pointed across the landing. "Come on, I'll show you—I'm sure there's something in there that will work. Do you want to wake the others, or—"

"I'm up," Brigga mumbled. Her hair fanned across her face as she lifted her head from the pillow. "Gods, how early is it?"

"Five-forty . . . seven," I told her. "Janna?"

"Awake." My captain pushed herself up to sitting. "What are you saying about a closet?"

"Don't worry about it—I'll pull training clothes for both of you," I said. "Just get ready for yoga."

"Downward dog in thirteen minutes!" Kenzi called as she led me across the landing. She opened a door, revealing a *massive* wardrobe room.

"You can walk inside of it," I whispered.

"That's the idea." Kenzi laughed. "It's a *walk-in* closet."

"And *all of these* clothes are available?"

"Yup. The pledges do the merchandising, and the current class likes to do it by season. So winter stuff's here, swimsuits are in the summer section . . ." Kenzi pointed to a rack that held miniscule swatches of fabric. Gods. I was *never* going swimming here. "Fall stuff's over there, so grab anything else you might need for the season. And workout gear gets its own section because we do that year-round. Obviously."

"Obviously." On that, we could agree.

"Most of the yoga pants are one size, so any of those should work. For sports bras, you're definitely a large. Here's one." Kenzi plucked a black fabric scrap from a neatly folded pile. "I'm not sure about your roommates, but smalls and mediums are closer to the front."

"I'll grab them. And the pants, too. Thanks, Kenzi."

"Any time. I'll meet you downstairs in a few minutes." Kenzi folded her hands together and bowed slightly. "Namaste."

"Right." I copied her pose, tucking my new almost-a-top over my arm as I bowed. "Namma-stay." Then I turned back to the pile of scraps, picked out training 'shirts' and pants for my teammates, and headed back to my room to dress for my first ever yoga class.

Here goes nothing.

Yoga was *hard*.

Despite Kenzi's self-proclaimed 'chill' demeanor and her deceptively soothing voice, she put us through a workout that rivaled Janna's cliff-climbing courses. We folded our bodies into unimaginable contortions, supported the entirety of our weight on one forearm and five toes, and stretched our limbs beyond the points I'd previously known them to be capable of. All the while, we channeled inner peace and mental quiet, and a stillness I most definitely *did not master* while trying to not fall over.

I was *totally* doing it again on Monday.

After a shower, breakfast, and a second tour of the castaway closet, this time with Janna and Brigga in tow, I was ready for my first full day at Southern California State. Morgan led us down the K. Mu steps, chatting excitedly about the folklore class we were scheduled to attend. As she spoke, I glanced at my seemingly ridiculous but era-appropriate outfit. I was decked out in black from head to toe, with a fitted sweater and pleated skirt that stopped a few inches above my knees. I wore my own high boots, since apparently, they were currently in fashion here. And I'd given in to Morgan's pleas, and let her wrangle my massive mane of crimson curls into a braided half-crown. She'd also insisted on doing our makeup, and we were all now sporting something called a 'cat eye.' Goddess Freya, who cruised around Asgard in a feline-driven chariot, would be proud.

Snort.

"Whoa, Ingrid. You're wearing a skirt?" Axel sauntered toward us, with Raynor at his side. They'd managed to find era-appropriate outfits—their castle must have had a castoff closet, too.

Heat filled my face as Axel's eyes roamed up and down my bare legs. *Stupid 'miniskirt.'*

"Did you wear that on purpose, or did someone force you to—oh, *hei* . . . uh . . ."

"Axel, Raynor, this is Morgan," I said quickly, grateful to shift the conversation away from my naked lower thighs. "She's in our folklore class, so she's showing us where to go."

"Folklore what?" Axel didn't take his eyes off my legs.

"Folklore class," I said loudly. Axel *finally* looked up. *Thank gods.* "You know, the one we're supposed to go to three days a week. Because we go to school here."

"Right. Your class." Raynor nodded slowly. "Yeah, we were going to ours too. Our class."

Beside me, Janna rolled her eyes. I couldn't blame her. We were pretty awful at this. But we were tired. And stressed. And no closer to tracking down the mysterious mage than we'd been ten hours ago. I'd run a quick test on the sample before falling into bed, but it hadn't turned up anything useful. I needed time to do a more thorough examination of the elements it contained . . . and a scientist to tell us where those elements might be found in Los Angeles. Though given the mage's preferred travel methods, they might be anywhere on the continent—in any era.

We had so much work to do.

"Wait." Morgan tilted her head. "You're the new exchange students in the Alpha house, right?"

"*Ja*," Axel answered. "Is that bad?"

"No. I'm just surprised you're heading to campus. Most of the Alphas schedule their classes so they have Fridays off. What do you have today?"

"Uh . . ." Raynor glanced at Brigga.

"He's with us," she blurted. "In folklore. They both are."

"No, they're not," I said quickly. "No, they're taking different classes. Right, Axel?"

Amusement danced in Axel's eyes. "No. We're definitely in that class. Three days a week, you and me. Folklore."

"Great." The word came out through gritted teeth.

"We can all walk together, then." Morgan smiled, oblivious to the irritation rolling off my tensed shoulders. "Don't you guys need your books, though? Or a notebook?"

"What for?" Raynor followed her down the road.

Brigga delivered a swift elbow to his ribs. "To take notes. In class."

"Oh." Raynor glanced at Axel. "We'll just remember everything."

Morgan shook her head. "I wish my brain worked like that."

"So do they." Janna chuckled as we hung a right and headed toward campus. "But these two have never been short on confidence. Speaking of, how was the rest of your night? Sounded like the party was still going strong after our curfew."

"Yeah." Axel grinned. "A big group of girls showed up a little before one. Brought a large container of mead with them; things got wild."

My stomach tightened. "Really?"

"That must have been the Deltas." Morgan pursed her lips. "Their house doesn't have a curfew. Or any standards, for that matter."

"Hey," Axel objected.

"No, I mean they don't have ethics rules—no standards chair there," Morgan said. "They're not particularly well respected on The Row. Not that it seems to bother them, much. Some of us are here for our BAs, and some are here for their M.R.S.'s."

I was too busy biting the inside of my cheek to try to decipher Morgan's code. "So, did you guys stay up with those girls, or . . . I mean, it was pretty late, you probably went to bed when they got there."

Axel's lips pulled up. "Oh, I *went* to bed."

Alone?

Stop it, Ingrid!

It was none of my business what Axel did in his bed. Or anywhere else, so long as it didn't compromise his dedication to our mission. And since right then, the mission demanded we sit through a folklore class without killing each other, I silenced my questions and followed Morgan into a massive building.

Without looking at Axel.

Morgan made her way down a crowded hallway. I

trailed behind her, trying not to gape at the sea of students. Valkyris Academy had been intimidating when I'd first arrived, but it was nowhere near this size. Our school had taken up just one quadrant of Valkryis' castle, and the student body numbered no more than a hundred—in the *entire* school. There were at least that many people in this hallway alone, each jostling to get into one of the doors that I presumed led to different classrooms. How big *was* this academy?

"Folklore's in here." Morgan opened one of the doorways and stepped inside.

Axel grabbed the door behind her, and held it open. "After you."

"Thanks." I kept my eyes straight ahead. As I passed Axel, he reached out and snagged my arm.

"Hey," he whispered. "You okay, shieldmaiden?"

"Never better," I said through a fake smile. "Now let me go."

Axel released his hold on my elbow. The heat immediately dissipated, leaving me with a feeling of . . . emptiness?

No. Not emptiness. Relief. Obviously.

Right.

I quickened my steps until I caught up with Morgan. She waved us into a middle row of the tiered classroom. The setup reminded me of the amphitheater back on Valkyris. A man I assumed to be the teacher stood at a podium on a low stage. He looked out at the roughly hundred-and-fifty seats, half of which were already filled with students.

"Must be Friday." He chuckled. "Do share today's lecture notes with your absent classmates, will you?"

"That's Professor Clark," Morgan sat in the center of the row. "He lectures for a while, then has us break into groups for theory discussions."

"This is a sitting class, then?" Axel dropped into the seat beside me. Janna, Brigga, and Raynor filled out the rest of the row.

"It's a lecture—if that's what you mean?" Morgan looked at him curiously. "Why? What are your classes like in Oslo?"

"Like this." I stared Axel down. "Right?"

"*Ja.*" He arched one brow. "Except the combat ones. Do you not have fighting classes here?"

Actually, he had a point. How did they defend their villages if they only ever sat through lectures?

"Fighting classes? Goodness, no." Morgan laughed as she pulled a textbook and notebook out of her bag. "We have PE, but those classes are more like lifting weights or playing volleyball. Sounds like you guys really hold onto those Viking roots in Norway."

She had no idea.

"If you are *all* of the students I'm getting today, I suppose we can get started." Professor Clark slid his eyeglasses over his nose. He was a kind-looking man, with thinning hair and an easy smile. "We've reached a turning point in our folklore—we're leaving the Greek tales behind, and transitioning to medieval England. Who here has heard of King Arthur?"

The majority of the students raised their hands.

"His story, though fictional, has always been one of my favorites. The boy who would be king was born a simple commoner, raised by a foster family, and never believed in his own greatness. Only with the help of his beloved, *revered*, clearly invaluable teacher—the great wizard and mage, Merlin—did Arthur grow into the wizened man who would one day lead his kingdom. I *do* hope Arthur appreciated his teacher—as, I'm sure, you do me."

The students near the front of the room laughed, but I was too hung up on one word to appreciate the joke.

"Did he say *mage*?" I glanced at Axel. The assassin's face was void of all amusement.

"He did." Axel confirmed. "Which means they *do* have them in this time—or at least, they've got them in their stories."

"Morgan?" Brigga leaned forward to whisper down the row. "When did this Arthur live?"

Morgan glanced at her textbook—a considerably sturdier one than the leather-bound parchments we had back home. "I believe this story took place in the fourteenth century. Not sure if there was a real Arthur though."

"Huh." I scribbled a note on my pad.

"What are you thinking?" Axel whispered.

"Just wondering how many mages are out there." I shrugged. "And hoping our time-traveling dark one doesn't meet up with any from the past . . . or the future."

"That guy called Merlin a 'great' mage." Axel jutted his chin at the professor. "Maybe there are light ones out there."

"He also said this was a fictional story." I raked my bottom lip between my teeth. "Doubt it's going to be much help."

"You never know." Axel shrugged. His shoulder brushed against mine, and I leaned away from the touch.

Focus, Ingrid.

"Merlin's teachings were unconventional, as all the best mage's are. He transformed Arthur into various animals, gave him practical lessons for his future life as King of England. Most notably, Merlin taught Arthur the danger of the rule of might—using one's power and strength to control others. According to Merlin, the only true reason to go to war is to prevent another war. Strength must be used to raise others up—not to force them into subjugation, or to bend their wills to your own."

"Sounds like he'd have fit right in back home," Janna whispered.

I nodded in agreement.

"Now, Merlin *did* see good in the use of might. He taught Arthur that he could harness this innately destructive human instinct for the betterment of mankind. By channeling might into a means of enforcing what's right, Arthur could promulgate the good, chivalrous code embodied by his Knights of the Round Table. Let me give you some examples."

Professor Clark pressed a button on the podium, and a word-covered rectangle lit up behind him.

"What's that?" I whispered to Morgan.

"The smart screen?" She wrote a header on her notepad. "Cool technology, huh? Some big donor gave the school money to put them in all the classrooms."

Technology? Back home, we would have called this magic. Did Morgan's people create all of this themselves? *Without älva dust?*

The teacher's voice pulled me back. For the next twenty minutes, Professor Clark explained the politics of Arthur's Round Table, the policies its knights enforced, and the way Merlin was able to influence his charge throughout his reign. When our teacher finished, he set his glasses on the podium and smiled at the class.

"That's enough talk from an old man. For the remainder of our time together, I'd like you to break into groups and discuss the policies *you* would enforce if you were tasked with creating a modern-day Round Table. What issues our society faces, and how might chivalry and kindness be applied to resolve those concerns. We'll circle back with some of your thoughts in a bit. Begin."

Uh . . .

"Billy, you guys want to work with us?" Morgan tapped the shoulder of a male in front of her.

He turned around. "Oh, hey, Morgan. How's it going?"

"Good. You guys ready for our exchange next weekend?"

"Nearly." Billy jabbed his thumb at his neighbor. "We just need Kyle to finish up the decorations."

"I never said I'd decorate anything." Kyle glanced back with a frown. "Hey, Morgan."

"Hi, Kyle." Morgan turned to me. "Billy and Kyle are co-social chairs for the Xi house. Guys, this is Ingrid, Janna, and Brigga—our exchange students from Norway."

"Norway?" Kyle's frown reversed. His gaze slid down our row before settling on me. "Well, hello there."

Heat flooded my neck. With his brunette waves and blue eyes, Kyle wasn't unattractive. But I was on a mission. And something about Kyle's arrogant grin made me think he wasn't the kind of guy who'd understand I needed to focus on work.

I shot my captain an uneasy look.

"*Hei*," Janna said calmly. "Kyle, is it?"

"'Sup?" Kyle raised his chin without taking his eyes off me.

Jana cleared her throat. "These are our friends from back home—Axel and Raynor."

"Hey." Billy nodded. "You guys Greek?"

"They're in the Alpha house," Morgan confirmed.

"I thought I saw you coming out of there this morning." Billy picked up his notebook. "Were you the one with the Delta twins on both arms?"

I nearly choked on a cough. *Oh, my gods. Was he?*

"That sounds like Axel." Raynor laughed.

Axel shot him a dark look. "Not this time."

"Ah." Billy shrugged. "Well, either way. Wanna tackle Carter's question?"

"What was the question?" Axel asked gruffly.

"The issues facing our society," Billy said. "And how the Arthurian policy of using might for right could be applied to implement change."

"God, do we start at the top of the issues list or the bottom?" Morgan sighed. "America's a mess."

"Every generation says that." Billy pointed out. "And every generation implements change."

"Chivalrous change could do us a world of good." Morgan picked up her own writing tools. "Okay, I'll be notetaker. Billy, kick us off."

For the rest of class, the two of them walked us through the concerns they felt an Arthurian model could best correct. From women's rights to representation in media—which I learned was the future version of Valkyris' oral poets—my team and I got a crash course in the issues facing our contemporary counterparts. It turned out that this place wasn't all that different from our home. Each of our cultures wanted to make our world the best possible version of itself. And while it may not have been practical to implement a benevolent knighthood like in the folktale, it was good to know our eras weren't that different after all. And it was a *huge* relief to discover they had at least some basic knowledge of mages in the current time.

Now we just had to figure out how to track one.

CHAPTER 8

WE SPENT THE BULK of the afternoon in one of the school's ten libraries. Morgan pointed us to the smallest one, claiming it had the best selection of the books we were looking for—stories about Merlin, Arthur, and the collective folklore surrounding mages. We needed background to figure out how magic-wielders operated. The concept wasn't foreign to us—we had *älva* back home, and the faeries' dust powered many of the otherwise inaccessible 'perks' of life in Valkyris. But the magic we knew was one-hundred-percent light, whereas our target operated in darkness. We had to understand how he was functioning if we wanted to stand a chance of stopping him. And, according to our disseminator, a library was the best place to learn.

"Here it is—the Merlin section." Brigga led us down a row framed with hard-spined texts. "Everybody grab a few, and see what you can find."

"These are labeled *Arthurian Legends*." Raynor frowned.

"That's what we're looking for." Brigga rolled her eyes. "Were you even paying attention in class?"

"You said we were looking for *Merlin*?" Axel folded his arms.

"That's why you should always take notes." Brigga shook her head. "Just flip through the pages and see if you can find any references to Merlin, or mages, or magic. Ooh, there's a table of contents in this one. That should make it easy. Here, Raynor." She thrust the book at him.

"Did she just call me dumb?"

"If the shield fits." I snickered, then pulled a handful of texts from a shelf before heading to one of the tables in the back. We read in silence for close to an hour, at which point I leaned back in my chair and rubbed my eyes.

If I have to stress out, this is a pretty nice place to do it.

The library was a gorgeous building—two stories of white stones and stained glass, with arched ceilings that made it look almost like a church. Students were clustered at dark, wood tables, or tucked into comfortable chairs staggered around the fireplace. Some looked relaxed, others flustered, but all understood the unspoken code of library silence.

All except for Axel Andersson.

"Here's something," he said loudly. He promptly earned a trio of *shushes* from the girls at the table in front of us. One of them turned around, her glare quickly morphing into awe as she gazed at Axel's arms. To be fair, they were slightly spectacular.

No, they're not. They're dumb.

Right.

"Sorry," Axel said, this time quieter. His dimple popped, and the girl giggled before turning back around.

Typical.

"What did you find?" I asked.

"According to this book, wizards—mages, to us— used to be really common," Axel recapped. "Pretty much every kingdom had at least one, with the most powerful usually serving as the king's personal advisor."

"Really?" Brigga asked, her interest clearly piqued. "So at one point magic-wielders were . . . everywhere?"

"Sounds like it." Axel glanced at the text. "But then there was some kind of a war between the dark wizards and the light ones. Apparently, there was going to be an astronomical anomaly, one that was supposed to create a surge of power. The light mages wanted to harness it to protect Earth, and the dark ones wanted to . . . oh, man."

"What?" I asked.

"They wanted to use it to open portals to other realms. Bad ones." Axel let out a low whistle. The girls at the nearby table looked over their shoulders and giggled.

Weren't they supposed to be studying?

"Bad ones like Helheim?" Janna asked.

"They don't mention any names. But wherever these places were, they had *fire monsters of death?*" Axel looked up.

"Muspelheim." I shuddered.

"Could be. Doesn't seem like whoever wrote this was familiar with the realms though. He didn't mention Asgard once." Axel put the book down, its pages facing upward.

"Maybe they have a different name for the gods' home." I tapped the text. "So what happened with the battle?"

"The two groups basically obliterated each other," Axel said. "They each cast spells, and within minutes, nearly all of them were dead. The ones who survived retreated into seclusion—and from the sound of it, they were never heard from again."

"What about the power surge?" Raynor asked. "Did either side manage to harness anything?"

Axel glanced at the pages. "There was a huge crystal near the battlefield. One of the surviving mages—it's not clear which side he was on—channeled the energy from the alignment into that stone. Then he shattered it into a dozen pieces, and scattered them across the land."

My brows shot to my forehead. "So there are twelve astronomically charged crystals out there somewhere, that every mage *ever* died trying to collect?"

"Pretty much." Axel reached up to stroke his neatly trimmed beard.

"But this is folklore," Janna said. "Right?"

"To these people." Raynor tilted his head at the neighboring tables.

"And to us?" Janna asked.

"Let's just say we put a lot more stock in *folklore* than they do. Look what I found in one of the books I pulled." Raynor held up a thin, glossy booklet. It was covered in drawings, with four big, bubbly letters splayed across the top—THOR.

"What is that?" I stared.

"It says it's a *comic*." Raynor set it on the table. "Seems to be a story with the God of Thunder as the main character. Apparently in this time, they think our deity is a hammer-wielding . . . what's a superhero?"

"A really good hero?" Brigga guessed. She slid the comic closer to her, and paged through it. "They think Thor has a girlfriend. And she isn't Sif."

"Do they not know him?" I peered across the table.

"Apparently not. This isn't an *edda*—it's a fictional account." Brigga passed the book back to Raynor. "If Thor is fictional here, and Merlin is just a legend . . . is it possible they don't believe in magic?"

"Plenty of people in our time don't understand magic." Janna pointed out.

"No. But they believe it exists," I countered. "Look around this place. They have flameless candles and bucketless baths and magic screens in their classrooms —all things we'd use *älva* dust to create back home. But they make everything themselves. Technology has surpassed magic. Or maybe it's replaced it entirely."

"What are you saying?" Axel asked.

"I'm saying . . . I don't think books are going to give us our answers. These people may write stories about mages and gods, but they don't believe in them. Look at this." I slid my book to the middle of the table. "This story about the lady of the lake—apparently, she's the wizard/mage/whatever who killed Merlin."

"She killed him? Why?" Brigga asked.

"I guess he fell in love with her and she just wasn't that into him?" I shrugged. "Anyway, she lived in some lake that had lotus-like flowers blooming in its sediment. Which I think is neat, because I didn't know flowers could bloom underwater. But whoever read this book before us wasn't impressed, or didn't believe it, because . . ."

I pointed to the handwritten words beside the text. *Lame. Dumb. Batman was better.*

"What's a Batman?" Raynor whispered. Brigga just shrugged.

"Are they talking about the flowers? Or the legend? Or the lake lady?" Axel asked.

"All? Who knows?" I closed the book. "My point is, nobody here seems to take any of this seriously. What we're researching as fact . . . all of that's just a story to them."

"That may be." Raynor glanced down at his book. "But somebody sure took *this* piece seriously. It's a spell —one designed to take over the world."

"What? Where?"

"Here." Raynor turned the book around so we could

all look at it. Sure enough, the top of the page read, *A Spell To Control Mankind And All The Realms.*

"Whoa," Janna whispered. "It lists ingredients I've never heard of. Quanta crystal? Illy bloom?"

"And ingredients we'll never identify. The bottom half have been crossed out." Brigga frowned at the blacked-over lines of text. "Why would someone do that to a book?"

"Maybe they didn't want anyone to perform the spell." Axel frowned.

"Nobody here believes in magic," I reminded him. "Remember?"

"Somebody must," Raynor said. "They made sure this spell never saw the light of day."

"More likely they got bored and decided to deface the library's property." I sighed. "Let's face it—magic is dead here. Or, at least, people seem to think it is. We aren't going to find a book to teach us how a dark mage operates, or what we can be doing to track him."

Axel leaned forward on his elbows. "Then we need to change tack. We might be able to get some idea of where our target's hiding if we can figure out why he's here."

"To bring chaos and destruction." Janna stared at Axel. "I thought that was obvious."

"I mean why is he *here*? In Los Angeles. A thousand years ahead of where he should be." Axel untied his hair from its bun, and raked his fingers through the strands. I *absolutely* did not pick up on the way the brown waves perfectly framed his face.

"As opposed to five hundred years earlier? And closer to home?" Raynor asked.

"Exactly. Think about it—he had a pretty good deal going back where we were. He had dragons to reanimate, and legions of dead warriors to lead, and from what I can tell, a considerably more manageable planet to attempt to control." Axel tapped his finger on the table. "There has to be a reason he's on the other side of the world at this point in time. What's in it for him?"

I turned to Janna. "Freia didn't have any idea why he time jumped?"

"If she did, she didn't tell me." Janna smoothed the arm of her sweater. "My instructions were to capture the mage and return him to Valkyris. Ideally, before he caused any damage to this world—or ours."

I nodded. "Then we'd better figure something out. It's already been a day—Odin only knows what he's done since he took off last night."

"Did you scan the sample we collected?" Raynor asked.

"*Ja*. But only quickly, and I didn't see anything out of the ordinary," I said. "I'll do a more thorough examination this weekend."

"I'll help you," Axel promised. "The guy in the room next to ours is a teaching assistant for one of the science departments. He mentioned that he had to go into the lab tomorrow—maybe he'll let us join him. If their technology's so advanced here, it's bound to be more useful than what you've got in your kit."

"Uh . . ." Spending my Saturday morning with Axel

was the dead last thing I wanted to do. But he had a point about technology. And the mission came first—always. "Sounds good."

BONG!

The chime of the wall clock pulled my attention.

"Shoot," Janna swore. "It's already five o'clock. Think our 'sisters' will notice if we skip . . . whatever tonight's social obligation is?"

"Lexi will," Brigga said drily. "She needs to get out more."

"Seriously." I closed my notebook. "Janna, what's our strategy for the next twenty-four hours?"

"Everybody, grab a few books to take home," she instructed. "I'm aware that mages are relegated to fiction here, but you never know what you might find. After . . . whatever tonight's house events are, log in a few hours of reading. Ingrid, you and Axel work on analyzing the sample first thing in the morning. Brigga, Raynor, and I will do some research in the field—we'll ask around to see if anyone's seen anything out of the ordinary. Maybe there's been a light surge every night from a certain location, or all the crops in a nearby region are dying or . . . *something* that could signal our target's whereabouts."

"Sounds like a plan." I picked up the texts I hadn't read. Beside me, Axel stretched his long legs.

"Do *you* know what your 'social obligation' is tonight?" he asked as we walked out of the library.

"House dinner, then some exchange with a fraternity. I'm not sure which one." I shivered as we stepped into the early evening chill.

"Are you cold?" Axel shifted his books to his right arm and shrugged his left arm out of his sweater. "Here, take my—"

"I'm fine. But thanks." I picked up my pace. "I'm just not used to these clothes."

"Mmm." Axel lengthened his stride until he reached my side. "I can't say I mind them. It's a good look on you, shieldmaiden."

I opened my mouth, prepared to snap back with a sharp retort. But the look on Axel's face was surprisingly sincere, and the words froze on my tongue.

I couldn't figure Axel out. One minute he was flirting with Lexi, and the next he was offering me his sweater. Either he was a total cad, or a sometimes gentleman. But no way could he be both.

Could he?

You don't have time for this right now. You need to focus on the mission.

I shoved all thoughts of Axel from my mind as I marched determinedly toward the sorority. There would be plenty of time for stewing later. I had a job to do.

And I wasn't about to let my team down.

CHAPTER 9

"*GOD MORGEN*, SUNSHINE." AXEL'S throaty voice boomed from the Kappa Mu foyer. I cleared the last stair, and adjusted my pack on my shoulder.

"Morning." I glanced toward the dining room. "Have you eaten? I was just going to grab one of those round bread things. Uh . . ."

"Bagels?" Axel offered.

"How do you know what they are?"

"We have a spread at our house, too." He strode toward the dining room. "We also have coffee. Do you have coffee here?"

"Of course we do." Lexi sauntered into the room. "Good morning, Axel. Inga."

"Ingrid," I corrected.

"Whatever." Lexi waved one hand. "Axel, would you like me to get you some coffee? We have takeaway cups if you're heading out. I was actually going for a walk myself. Maybe we could—"

"Thanks for the offer, but I've got a study date with Ingrid." Axel grinned.

My cheeks flushed at his choice of words.

"Date?" Lexi's eyes narrowed.

"We have to study," I clarified. "Come on, Axel. Let's get out of here."

"What about my coffee?" He looked longingly at the counter.

"Grab it and go." I folded my hands together.

"You want any?" he offered.

"No. But snag me a bagel."

"Will do."

While Axel retrieved my breakfast and filled one of the cups in the takeaway pile, Lexi shot me a death glare. I stared back coolly, refusing to blink.

She rolled her eyes as Axel turned around, then treated him to her most beatific smile. "See you around, Axel." She waggled her fingers as she pranced over to the bread table.

"See you." Axel took a slug of his drink, wincing as the liquid hit his mouth. "It's hot."

"So I gather. Come on." I snatched the bagel from his hand before scaling the three steps that led from the dining room to the foyer. I took a bite, then headed toward the front door. Outside, brilliant beams streamed from a radiant sky. It was a beautiful, November day.

One I was happy I'd worn pants in.

"No skirt today?" Axel glanced at my fabric-covered knees. "That's a shame."

"I dug through the castaway closet again last night," I said. "Apparently they're super into *jeans* now. I have to say, they're pretty comfortable."

"Not really my thing." Axel's gaze dropped to his own pants—a sporty pair with a triangular emblem on the upper thigh. "But they look good on you. The top's a nice touch."

"*Ja*, well." I smoothed the front of sweater. The Greek letters for Kappa Mu were embroidered on the front in a starry fabric. "House pride, and all that."

"Sure." Axel took another hit of coffee as he led me to the edge of the lawn. An athletic-looking guy in an outfit similar to Axel's stood near the road. "Hey, Chase. This is my friend Ingrid. Thanks for letting us use your lab."

"It's the chemistry department's lab." Chase grinned. "And I'm always happy to make more science friends. Are you a chem major too, Ingrid?"

"I'm just taking general classes," I demurred. "My background's mostly in . . ." *Combat.* ". . . physical stuff."

"Ah. Physiology and kinesiology are side passions of mine." Chase flexed his arm. "Gotta know how to maximize efficiency in the gym if you want to get results. Am I right?"

If Axel was as confused as I was, he didn't show it. He just nodded and said, "Totally."

Okay then.

"Do you always work this early on Saturdays?" I

adjusted my pack, then took another bite as I followed Chase down the road.

"Yeah. I have a standing session group for first-year chemistry students. This week, we're going over a lab that was particularly tough for them." Chase rounded the corner, and headed toward campus. "Being a TA is fun—it's cool to see the light bulbs go on when you're tutoring newbies, you know?"

"I do." Axel's dimple deepened. "I was Ingrid's tutor back home. You could say I taught her everything she knows."

"Hardly," I snorted. "I excelled *despite* your instruction."

"You can tell yourself that, but there's no way it's true."

"It *is*," I snapped. "Your approach was completely off base for someone of my stature. A dart-and-weave attack is *far* more effective than charging in like a bull."

Axel shrugged. "My strategy's worked out just fine for me. Just ask Freia."

"Sorry, what did you say you guys studied back in Oslo?" Chase's brows formed a deep *V*.

I glared at Axel. "Physical . . . education?"

"Uh-huh." Chase chuckled. "Well, glad to have you on the science team. For now at least. Lab's up ahead— first floor in the white building, second door on the left. Help yourself to any of the supplies in there. I'm going to grab a coffee first."

"Thanks," I called as Chase walked toward a cart boasting 'LA's Best Coffee!'

Huh.

When we reached the white building, Axel held open the door. I polished off the rest of my bagel as I slipped past him and made my way into the chemistry lab. It was a massive, sterile room filled with glossy, black tables and enough test tubes and burners to fill an entire barn back home. Axel hadn't been wrong about the technology . . . though he had been way off about his influence on my fighting skills.

"Your ego's really gone to the next level," I observed as I pulled the sample from my pack. "You really had no idea how to teach a girl to fight."

"I didn't treat you like a girl because I didn't see you as one." Axel grabbed a handful of supplies from a nearby table, and carried them back to ours.

"Gee, thanks."

"I mean it. From the day I rescued you from Clan Bjorn—"

"Excuse me," I corrected. "But I rowed your sorry butt away from my captors. You know, after you injured yourself trying to 'rescue' me."

"*Ja*, that didn't exactly go the way I planned. Makes a good story though, doesn't it?" Axel placed a row of tubes into a holder, and turned his attention to sorting strips of test paper. If we could determine the acidity of our sample, we should be able to ascertain more information about its origin.

"If you're okay telling your friends that we met when you tried to save me from an evil clan, got yourself injured, lost your dragon, and couldn't even row your own boat home, then sure. It's a *great* story."

"As I was saying." Axel collected a handful of droppers. "From the day I *assisted* in rescuing you from Clan Bjorn —as I concede you played a role in rescuing yourself."

"And saving you, too," I pointed out.

Axel ignored me. "From that first encounter, you showed me you were no girl. You were a warrior. One who was determined to earn a spot on the Shield-maiden Squadron."

"And I did it," I said proudly. "No thanks to your 'grab the heaviest sword and swing as hard as you can' suggestions."

"It's called Socratic teaching," Axel countered. "And it worked. You found the blade size that worked best for you, and you developed a technique that earned you a spot on the squadron on your first tryout. Nobody makes it their first time, Ingrid. Nobody."

"I made it because I worked my butt off," I said. "Every minute I wasn't in classes, I was going over combat sequences or conditioning."

"I know." Axel's lips quirked up. "Who do you think made sure the training room was always available when you needed it?"

My eyes narrowed. "If you're trying to take credit for my work ethic, you've got—"

"What I'm trying to do . . ." Axel pressed his palms to the table, ". . . is tell you that I've been on your side from day one. So, why do you hate me?"

My hands tensed. "I don't hate you."

"You sure act like it." Axel leaned forward. "You rarely make eye contact, you move away whenever I walk next to you, and you do everything in your power to *not* be alone with me."

"We're alone now," I objected.

"And you'd rather be anywhere but here. I saw your face when I offered up lab time this morning—you looked miserable."

"*Ja.* Well . . ."

Axel lowered his head so our eyes were level. It took everything I had not to look away from his stare . . . or punch him in his intense, too-perfect face.

"What's your deal, Ingrid?"

"Excuse me?"

He leaned even closer. "What exactly did I do to you?"

I blanched. It wasn't what he'd done to *me*—it was what he'd done to countless girls before me. I'd only been in Valkyris for a year, but during that time my friends had told me about *all* of Axel's romantic conquests. From the daughters of the governing families, to the women who'd thrown themselves at him on missions, to my own classmates back at the academy. The captain of Valkyris' Airborne Assassins had made his way through most of the females on our home island . . . and beyond.

Why would I want to have anything to do with him?

And how could I explain without making him think

I was jealous of all the girls who'd come before me? *Which I wasn't.*

Are you sure?

"You and I are just different," I blurted, silencing the stupid voice in my head. "You get anything"—*and anyone*—"you want at the snap of your fingers. I've had to work for every single thing that was worth having, from my place in Valkyris, to my spot on the squadron. Now put those test strips into the tubes, and we'll siphon trace amounts of the sample into the glass. Without touching it." I passed Axel one of the leather gloves I'd found on the supply table.

He slipped it onto his left hand, his eyes softening as he looked at me.

"What?" I couldn't keep the irritation from my voice.

"How are you doing with everything?" Axel asked quietly. "With your . . . family."

"I am here on a mission," I said determinedly. "I do not want to talk about my family."

"You *never* talk about your family, so far as I know," Axel said cautiously. "Don't you want to work through some of your . . ."

"My what, Axel? My disappointment that my mother did *nothing* to protect me my entire life? My anger that my father handed me off to the most brutal clan in Norway in order to save our tribe? My disappointment that he didn't realize the error of his ways until just before he died? What exactly would you have me work through?"

"Everything," Axel said gently. "I'd have you work through every one of those feelings. They're all yours, Ingrid. And they all deserve to be witnessed so that you can heal."

"I'm healed just fine. Now hand me one of those tubes. In case you've forgotten, we're on the job."

Axel picked up one of the glass cylinders. As he passed it to me, our fingertips brushed. I ignored the spark that shot along my arm.

"I get where you're coming from," Axel said quietly. "But if you ever do want to talk—"

"Pass me the solvent." I pointed to the small container into which I'd poured a blue liquid. I was done with . . . with whatever Axel was trying to do. I just wanted to identify the compounds, and track down our target.

Without Axel's inquisition.

Two hours later, we'd narrowed the specimen's contents to a pair of primary compounds. The first was a hydrogen-based substance—one my reference guide informed me was commonly found in coastal plants.

"You're saying it contains . . . milk weed?" Axel's lips turned down.

"Miquelianin. I think." I looked up from the textbook I'd pulled from a shelf behind the professor's desk. "At least, that's what those elements seem to add up to in here."

"What the Helheim's miquelianin?"

"This says it's a compound found in certain plants, vegetables, and . . . wine."

"Maybe the dark mage is a drunk." Axel smirked.

"Entirely possible. But it's also consistent with our other primary compound. Whatever this residue comes from, it seems to be some kind of a plant."

"Interesting." Axel stroked his jaw. "What's the secondary compound? The one you said there were only trace elements of?"

"That's harder to ascertain." My eyes shifted between my notebook and the text. I flipped pages until I came to the one I'd flagged, then re-read my notes. "It's definitely from a crystal—one with a composition similar to quartz, I think. But it's not an exact match. There's something else in there—it's making the elements react unpredictably. Watch."

Using my glove, I withdrew a drop of the sample from the test tube. Then I divided it into two small segments on a glass plate.

"According to this textbook, the chemical composition of quartz is sulfur dioxide—one part silicon and two parts oxygen. Most acids won't have much of an effect on quartz, but one will—hydrofluoric acid. That particular substance dissolves the crystal. Or, it *should*."

I pulled another dropper from a glass beaker. When I deposited its contents onto the plate, the original drop vibrated, then took on a luminescent shimmer.

"I'm assuming that was hydrofluoric acid?" Axel arched one brow.

"Correct."

"And the quartz did *not* dissolve."

"Precisely." I returned the dropper to the beaker, and moved on to the second drop. "Now, the book says that normally with sulfur dioxide, application of a base will create a silicate—a salt. But here . . ."

I repeated my earlier experiment, this time drawing a drop from a different beaker. When I placed it on the slide, the original liquid turned black and evaporated.

"I take it there's no such thing as a gaseous salt?" Axel said drily.

"There may well be—Valkyris is way behind Los Angeles in technology, and probably research, too," I said. "But gaseous is not the state that usually results from this particular application at this particular temperature."

Axel shook his head. "What's your thinking?"

"I think the crystal was altered on an imperceptible level—though because its structural integrity is intact, I can't ascertain *how*." I placed the dropper back in the beaker. "What I do know is this particular quartz sample is unlike any I've seen before. I'd love to know where it came from."

"*Ja . . .*"

"And why it's behaving unpredictably." I wrote down my findings in my notebook, and slid it into my bag. "We might as well call it for the day. We have a lot to work with—miquelianin, non-compliant quartz, water-based plant compounds . . ."

"Sounds like he's drawing power from water

sources." Axel picked up the test tubes and carried them to the sink. "Good thing one of us is *extremely* familiar with water."

And, there it was. The great Axel ego.

"What *aren't* you familiar with?" I rolled my eyes.

"Not much," Axel said confidently. "I'm a skilled assassin, master dragon wrangler, and, under normal circumstances, an extraordinary seaman."

"Unless you need a girl to row you home." I couldn't help myself.

"Girls can be excellent rowers. " Axel shrugged. "My mother taught me everything I knew. She was an accomplished sailor. She captained voyages for Freia and Halvar in Valkyris' early years."

I paused halfway to the sink. Axel had never mentioned his parents. "Oh?"

"*Ja*. In the beginning, secrecy was the key to Valkyris' survival. Freia sent my parents on a lot of scouting trips. They mapped out the coastal geography, and created a breakdown of tribal boundaries and allegiances. It's what we used to evade detection during the first days of Valkyris' existence."

I carefully poured out the contents of my beakers, and filled the sink with suds. "Were you born on Valkyris then, or . . ."

Or were you rescued, like me?

"I was born there." Axel joined me at the sink. "Halvar and my father had crossed paths in their old tribes, and when my parents caught wind of what the Halvarssons were creating, they wanted in. They helped establish Valkyris, and they were its fiercest protectors until . . ."

My breath caught in my chest as Axel's gaze dropped. Without thinking, I reached out to touch his arm. "I'm sorry you lost them."

"*Ja.* Me too." He looked up with a sad smile. "I was fifteen when they took their final voyage. They were only supposed to be gone for two weeks, but a month passed, then two. Then a year."

"Axel . . ." My fingers wrapped lightly around his shoulder.

"Freia and Halvar took me in. They put me up in a room right down the hall from theirs, and they told me to consider them my family. It wasn't a huge stretch since Erik was already pretty much a brother to me. Raynor, not so much."

"Did you ever find out what happened to your parents?"

"No." Axel turned to the sink, and scrubbed a beaker clean.

I reluctantly let my hand drop.

"I like to think they're in Valhalla, helping Asgard fight for the good of mankind."

"I'm sure they are," I said softly.

"That's why I'm so good at my job."

"Why's that?"

"None of us can know how much time we have. But we can control what we do with that time—how hard we work, how many people we help, whether we leave the world a little bit better than we found it. My parents came to Valkyris so that I could have the chance to live a better life than the one they were born into. I've never known anything else, but I see what it's like in the rest of our world. And I want to do for that world what my parents did for me—fight to extend that same opportunity to live in honor, valor, and dignity, to every single person who wants it."

My chest tightened at Axel's words. "That's why I fought so hard for a spot on the Shieldmaiden Squadron," I said. "I didn't want any other girls to have to live like I did—back home in my parents' tribe, or as captives of clans like Bjorn."

"I know," Axel said quietly. "That's the reason I made sure you got the training you needed to earn that spot."

I opened my mouth to call him out on his arrogance. But the words caught in my throat as I took in Axel's intense stare. While I knew darned well I'd earned that spot through my own blood, sweat, and tears, I couldn't deny that I *had* needed someone to show me the ropes at Valkyris Academy. And, for better or worse, Axel had been my teaching assistant.

"Right. Well, thanks." I tore my gaze away from Axel's emerald-green gaze, and resumed washing our materials. "If we're done here, we should get our findings back to the team."

"Sure." Disappointment clouded Axel's voice. I glanced up to find him staring at me, his eyes tinged with sadness. Was he thinking about his parents, or the realities of our world, or something else entirely?

As quickly as I'd registered it, the look was gone. Axel turned his back to me, and cleared the rest of our workspace. We cleaned in silence, then walked the short distance to our respective houses. There, we filled our friends in on what we'd discovered about the sample. But I couldn't help but think that I'd discovered something even more surprising than a compromised crystal.

Axel and I aren't that different after all.

CHAPTER 10

T HE REST OF THE weekend was an exercise in restraint. My friends had been successful with their fieldwork, learning that not only had Thursday night's statue destruction *definitely* been noticed by the students of Southern California State, but that those students had also observed a handful of unusual occurrences in the week before we'd arrived. Our dark mage had been busy destroying landmarks around the Los Angeles area, from a metal dinosaur in the remnant of some tar pit, to one of the letters on a giant hilltop sign that now read *HOLLYWOO*. The locals had written off the destruction as seismic episodes—apparently, this part of the world was prone to earthquakes, and mild destruction was a semi-regular occurrence. But my team suspected the anomalies might be something else entirely.

Now we just had to track the perpetrator down.

"What's the common thread?" I asked Janna as we

headed to our Monday morning astronomy class. We kept our voices low since Morgan walked a few steps ahead of us. Her schedule was nearly synched to ours, which made skipping class pretty much impossible.

"I have no idea," Janna murmured. "He destroyed the statue while he was trying to take you out—maybe someone else came after him at the tar pit and the Hollywood sign. He could have destroyed those trying to escape, too."

"Maybe." I slowed my steps so we fell farther behind Brigga and Morgan. "Or maybe he was looking for something in those locations. We already know there's a reason he's here, in this exact spot at this exact time. If he's tracking something, maybe he thought he'd found it in the pit. Or by the sign."

"Or maybe he's just got an anger problem." Janna sighed. "We could do this all day. But we'd better hurry up—Morgan keeps looking back here and you know how she likes to—"

"What are you two talking about?" Morgan turned around with a smile.

"Ask questions," Janna muttered.

"Just how excited we are for today." I dialed my enthusiasm up a notch. Morgan had already told us astronomy was one of her favorite classes. From the way she now beamed at the bevy of attractive boys streaming into the science building, I had a guess as to why.

"Professor Stinoa is really engaging," Morgan bubbled. "She presents constellations as stories, and always has something to share about how they were viewed by ancient civilizations. Did you know, ancient warriors used the Big Dipper as an entrance test? If you could spot which star was the double, then your eyesight was good enough to be an Aztec fighter! Or maybe it was a Roman fighter. It's kind of hard to remember. I'll look it up."

She opened the classroom door, and we followed her inside. This one had another stadium setup, with rows of tiered seats looking down on the stage-top podium where Professor Stinoa stood. She was young —no more than thirty, tops. And she was gorgeous in her fitted pants and a button-down sweater. Her long, black hair was tied up in a loose bun, and she had the appearance of a woman who was equal parts approach-able and smart.

No wonder the classroom was nearly full.

"Okay, everyone. Take your seats. I know the astro-nomical alignment's a big deal, but we can't start discussing all the ways it's going to change your life until you *sit. Down.*" Professor Stinoa clapped her hands on the last two words.

"Astronomical alignment?" I followed Morgan, Brigga, and Janna down a packed row. We had to climb over a sea of legs to get to the four empty seats at the end.

"Do you not know about it?" Morgan pulled out her notepad. "Yeah, it's been a big thing in the news for the last few weeks. At least, it has in California. All of the planets are going to be in the same part of the sky soon.

And since everyone here's into energy and flow and chi and all of that, and the vibrational alignments will resonate throughout the entire solar system, maximizing their strength . . . well, it's kind of a thing."

Janna's hand snaked around my wrist. "Morgan, how often do planets line up nowadays?"

"Now? Not sure. Probably the same as always." Morgan shrugged. "I'm sure Professor Stinoa will cover it in the lecture. Why? Do you think that's going to be on the test?"

"Maybe," Janna said lightly. I shot her a curious glance.

"Why are you asking about a timeline?" I whispered to my captain.

"Because," she whispered back. "We just read something about a planetary alignment. Remember?"

"I read a lot of things over the weekend." I pointed out. "You're going to have to be more specific."

"Shh." The girl in front of me turned around with a frown.

I sank lower in my seat with a muttered, "Sorry."

"If you're all done talking, I can *finally* begin." Our teacher activated the smart screen behind her. An image of multiple orbs appeared on the white wall. "As I was saying, we're going to see a very rare astronomical occurrence sometime in the next few months. While it's impossible for all eight planets to come into perfect alignment, on account of the tilt of their orbits and their orientation, we *will* see all of the planets in the same area of the sky for the first time in about twelve hundred years. Of course, this has scientists, astronomers, and yes, doomsday predicters, all atwitter."

I glanced at Janna. "Doomsday predicters?"

"Atwitter?" she whispered back.

"As always, we'll look at this subject from a cultural perspective first, and then a scientific one." Professor Stinoa rested her palms on the podium. "The last time the planets were this close together was roughly during the Viking era. Legends tell us that during the 'alignment'—again, we use that term loosely—the veil between the supernatural and earthly realms was lifted, and magic was transferred from the spirit world to ours. A series of energetic anomalies occurred, leading to the creation of 'magically charged' artifacts that, of course, have never been seen again."

Recognition nibbled at the back of my head. Something about that 'legend' sounded familiar . . . though I couldn't put my finger on exactly what.

"Then, a few hundred years' later, four of the planets fell into near-alignment again. These planets were said to have sent another charge at our Earth, creating a shift in a select group of minerals—super crystals, if you will. These hyper-charged stones were alleged to be imbued with traces of the same magic that was funneled to our planet during the Viking-era 'alignment.' Of course, nobody's ever seen these crystals either, and as scientists, we put no stock in silly legends." Professor Stinoa's eyes twinkled. "Right?"

"I want the magic rocks," a guy from the front row called out.

"I want the charged artifacts," the girl next to him countered. "Where were they supposed to have been left?"

"Again, it's pure subjection since these are merely *legends.*" Professor Stinoa's lips quirked up. "But the stories place the artifacts in the northern regions of Europe—most likely, Scandinavia."

"And the rocks?" asked the guy.

"Those are said to have been scattered across two regions—England, and the western part of North America—possibly even here in Los Angeles."

My heart thudded as the class broke into excited chatter.

"Here, in LA? Ohmigod, we *have* to find them."

"Dude. They're probably worth a cool mil. We could totally finance our film."

"Do you think they're too big to make into earrings?"

"Janna." I leaned closer to my captain. "This is it."

"What's it?" she whispered back.

"The reason our target is here. Now."

Brigga leaned in from Janna's other side. "He's here for the crystals."

"The ones from the story about the wizards," Janna said slowly. "The ones that were created in the battle that wiped the mages from our world."

"Exactly." I flipped my notebook to the page I'd been scribbling on over the weekend. "It didn't make any sense that our target showed up in a magic-less world. He had to be looking for something. If these rocks are legitimate . . . and if they carry even a trace of the power they're supposed to . . ."

Brigga's eyes widened. "We have to find them first," she blurted.

"You're going to try to find them?" Morgan looked up from her notes. *Oh, gods. How much did she hear?* "You do know the stones and the artifacts are just a myth, right? This was Professor Stinoa's cultural context discussion—not the scientific one."

"*Ja.*" I waved one hand. "We totally know. Brigga was joking. Weren't you, Brigga?"

Brigga nodded so enthusiastically, her blond braid bounced atop her shoulder. "Yes. Joking. Ha ha."

Seriously, she was the worst liar.

"Enough chatter." Professor Stinoa clapped her hands together. "Now that we've gone over the cultural foundations for this event, we can get into the scientific—*aka*, the *fact-based* applications—of what this planetary phenomenon will mean. It is notable that the predicted alignment wasn't scheduled to occur for another three to four hundred years. Something has shifted in our solar system, closing the projected timeline on the planet's orbits. Scientists noticed the shift in the past year, and have been struggling to find an objective cause. Some say it may come down to climate change, which has altered our planet's atmosphere and possibly had further-reaching implications than we could have realized. Others say an influx of meteors within the orbits of our solar system's innermost planets has pulled them slightly off course. And, of course, our new age friends say it's a sign of the end of the world, and we should prepare for the second coming of God, Zorp, Xanu, and/or Odin. Depending on your religious affiliation."

"Who's Xanu?" Brigga whispered.

The girl next to Morgan looked over with wide eyes. "You don't want to mess with him. He'll stick thetans to your root chakra and unground you for life. *For. Life!*"

What the actual Helheim?

"What we *do* know is that if its current rate of progression holds, the 'alignment' should take place near the end of the semester." Professor Stinoa spoke over the chatter. "With that in mind, we're going to take a field trip to the desert where light pollution is at a minimum and visibility will be optimal. I'll confirm once we're sure of the alignment's date, but for now tentatively keep the weekend of December thirteenth open."

"Saint Lucia's Day?" I blinked at Brigga. The date marked the observance of Valkyris' festival of light. "Think there's any significance to that?"

"I have no idea." She scribbled furiously in her notebook. "But there's a lot to digest, for sure. We have some idea of why our target's here—for the crystals, I'm guessing. And why he came now—the alignment. Though I don't know how he's planning to harness whatever comes from that."

"If the crystals *are* real, we've got to hunt them down before he can." I kept my voice low. "How do you find a crystal?"

"You're our tracker." Janna tapped her finger to on her desk. "Got any ideas?"

"Maybe." I paused. "Back home, the seers said crystals have energy traces—pulses you can see or feel or maybe smell? I don't know how it works. My friend Vidia learned about it in her final semester at the academy. She didn't explain much, so I never learned to do it myself. But maybe someone in our sorority studies magic rocks. The professor said everyone here's into energy, right?"

"*Ja* . . ." Janna's brows knitted together.

"Hey, Morgan?" I turned to my left. "Anybody in Kappa Mu know about crystals? Or study the whole energy thing Professor Stinoa was talking about?"

"Plenty," Morgan said confidently. "You should talk to Kayla and Kenzi. Their mom is a reiki master."

"A what-now?" I frowned.

"She's super into energy," Morgan translated. "And she knows how to shape it using crystals and flower essences and all kinds of stuff. The girls understand it pretty well—Kenzi's more into it than her sister. She uses it in her yoga classes sometimes."

"Thanks," I whispered. Then I nodded at Janna and Brigga. For the first time since we'd gotten here, I felt like we had a lead.

Now we just had to see where it took us.

CHAPTER 11

THE NEXT FEW DAYS passed uneventfully. We went to Kenzi's daily yoga classes, and spoke briefly with her about what she'd learned from her mom. The whole energy thing sounded *intense*, so I agreed to be our designated 'hippie,' as Kenzi called it. I'd spend time every day learning more about crystals and flowers and chakras from our sorority sister. If the best way to track our target was energetically, I wanted to be prepared.

In the meantime, Brigga and Raynor continued with the fieldwork. They asked everyone they came into contact with about unusual weather patterns, mysterious crystals, and whether they'd noticed anything out of the ordinary. And Axel and Janna read countless books, searching for anything that might lead us to a still-living mage, mysterious water-blooming plants, or the place the original crystals were scattered.

By the time Thursday night rolled around, we were

all exhausted. *Obviously.* Unfortunately for us, sleep was out of the question. Keeping our cover meant heading out for yet *another* social obligation—a bowling exchange with the Alphas. Apparently, the night would consist of hurtling a three-pound ball at a stack of innocent 'pins,' while consuming vast quantities of mead as per exchange tradition. But considering we had axe-throwing festivals back home, and the mead here was far less potent—or so Axel claimed—I figured I could hold my own.

Until Lexi sauntered into my bedroom.

"So, Ingrid." Her voice positively dripped with insincerity. "Are you and Axel, like, a thing?"

Brigga and Janna practically sprinted from their places at the bathroom mirror.

"What?" I stared at them.

"Are you?" Brigga blurted.

"No! Why would you think that?"

"Because you're always together," Lexi drawled. "I just figured . . . well, that's good. Then you won't mind if I move in on him."

"I thought you already did." I slipped my arms through the flowy sweater Kayla had loaned me. "Last week. Didn't he turn you down at that party?"

Lexi's eyes narrowed. "*Nobody* turns me down."

"Axel did," Brigga agreed. "You were pretty clear about what you were offering, and trust me—if he was interested, he'd have taken you up on it by now. He moves pretty fast."

Brigga would know.

"Did you ever think maybe *I* was playing it slow?" Lexi tossed her hair over her shoulder. "I don't know what it's like in Norway, but around here we don't just jump into bed with a guy the first night we meet him."

I choked back a cough. "Uh, right."

Lexi placed one hand on her hip. "What's that supposed to mean?"

"Nothing." I turned to the mirror over the dresser, and pulled the top half of my hair into a loose braid. "I really don't care what you do—in your bedroom, or anywhere else."

"Good." Lexi's lips pulled up in a satisfied smirk. "I just wanted to make sure I'm not stepping on my *sister's* toes when I hook up with that gorgeous Viking. These things can get . . . complicated, you know?"

"Mmm." I refused to bite.

"I really think you're wasting your time," Janna offered. "Brigga's right—Axel goes after what he wants. And based on what we saw last week, I don't think you're it. Sorry, Lexi."

"Please. *Everybody* wants this." Lexi gestured to her body. "See you on the bus."

Once she'd sauntered out of our room, I closed the door behind her and turned to my teammates. "What's a bus?"

"Oh my gods, Ingrid. *Are* you and Axel a thing?" Brigga plopped herself on my bed.

"I already told you, no." I crossed to the dresser and searched for a hair tie.

"*Ja.* But your face was bright red when you said it."

Janna pulled a cardigan from the closet and slipped it over her dress.

"Because Lexi's rude, and I don't like being around her." I secured my braid and grabbed a pair of low boots. "Booties is a ridiculous name for shoes, don't you think?"

"And now you're changing the subject." Brigga pursed her lips. "You *do* like him."

"I do not," I said firmly. "Axel Andersson has been nothing but a pain in my side since his botched attempt to rescue me and Vidia from Clan Bjorn. Not only did he get his dragon killed—which both offended the gods and created a world of trouble for your sister, may she rest in peace—but he got himself injured, and I had to row his sorry butt Odin only knows how many miles home."

Janna's brow quirked. "Where he made sure you had the best training, so you'd never be in a position of weakness again."

"Well . . . maybe. But—"

"And where he promptly dumped every other girl he was seeing, for reasons he never bothered to explain." Brigga crossed her arms.

"That had nothing to do with me. He's obviously a jerk who's bad at commitment."

"Is he?" Brigga stared at the ceiling. "I mean, I was definitely angry when things ended with us. I wasn't used to being broken up with. That's usually *my* job."

Bless her egocentric heart.

"But he was way less of a jerk after he came back

from Bjorn. Maybe it was his near-death experience, or maybe it was meeting you and Vidia and seeing everything you guys lived through there. Or maybe he was just finally ready to grow up a bit. I don't know."

"Don't we have a bowling studio to get to?" I zipped up my booties and stood.

"It's a bowling *alley*," Brigga corrected. "And nice subject change. Again."

"This conversation's over." I slid Freia's dagger into the small, leather backpack I'd snagged from the castaway closet, made sure the *älva* dust was still tucked safely in my nightstand drawer, smoothed the front of my grass-green dress, and wrenched open the door. "We don't want Lexi writing us up for tardiness. Or whatever offense she threatens us with today."

"I think a write-up is the least of your concerns." Janna slid one of her leather cuffs around her wrist. "Lexi's after Axel."

"Again, this affects me none."

"Then why are your cheeks pink?" Janna slipped a dagger into her own mini-backpack.

"They're not." I rolled my eyes. "Just drop it, all right? We have important things to focus on. Like blending in enough tonight to be able to sneak out for the weekend and look for our target."

"Blending in may require dancing." Janna's eyes twinkled. "I heard there's a dance facility called a *nightclub* attached to the bowling ballroom. Apparently, they play music there."

"Bowling *alley*," Brigga corrected again. "And yes. Meri said there would be dancing."

"Interesting," Janna said.

Brigga batted her eyes. "Maybe Ingrid can *not* be into Axel there."

"I *am* not into Axel!" I growled.

"Whatever you say." Brigga snagged her bag off the back of her chair and practically skipped down the stairs. It took everything I had not to reach out and trip her as she passed.

"She's getting on my last nerve," I muttered to Janna.

"She's just trying to help." Janna shrugged. "After all, she's been there. Though, who hasn't."

"Did you and Axel ever . . ."

"Oh, gods no." Janna shook her head. "Muscled-out assassin boys were never my type."

"No?" I followed her onto the landing. The sound of concentrated chatter rose from downstairs. "What is your type?"

Janna's lips quirked up as we walked down the stairs. "Definitely not Axel."

Well that was something.

"There you are!" Kayla's cheerful voice rang from the foyer. "I think you're the last two. K. Mus, everybody on the bus!"

The throng of girls chatted excitedly as they moved in a wave toward the front door. I leaned closer to Janna and whispered, "Again, what's a . . . bus?"

My stomach dropped as the wave pushed us toward

a massive steel box. It looked like one of the horseless wagons we'd seen on our first day here, but bigger.

And it was filled with Alphas.

The guys cheered as we walked down the aisle to take our seats inside the box. Axel and Raynor sat in the back, their calm expressions not betraying so much as a hint of anxiety. But they had to be apprehensive. This thing had no horse to pull it—and no dragon, either. From what little I'd gathered, it ran purely on a technology we neither understood nor had the ability to correct, should something go wrong. We were one hundred percent in the hands of the stranger helming the wheel. I was once again left with the feeling of being completely and totally out of control.

Which pretty much summed up my life.

Bowling was not for the faint of heart.

It took a solid two games before my ball didn't go straight for the gutter the minute it left my hand. Another full game passed before I could knock down more than three pins in any one try. After that, my arm was too sore to care how clumsy I looked launching myself along a slippery walkway in ugly, borrowed shoes.

I trained six hours a day back home, but this three-pound ball was doing a number on my triceps.

My only consolation was the fact that Janna and Raynor were even worse than me. Janna's ball lived permanently in the gutter though all four of our games, while Raynor somehow managed to jump his clear into the next lane. Twice.

"You're throwing it too hard." Brigga's instruction came through barely contained laughter. "Go easy. Just step forward and release. Like this." She demonstrated, her ball rolling easily down the center of the aisle.

"Strike!" Troy shouted. He'd volunteered to be the guys' third team member, evening out our sides and, unfortunately, helping them ensure an easy victory in our first four matches. Brigga was the only decent member of our team, while both Troy and Axel were admirably adept.

Jerks.

"I *tried* going easy," Raynor gritted out. "It went into the gutter and barely made it to the end zone."

"The pin deck?" Troy laughed. "End zone's for football, man."

"That's the one we watched over the weekend, *ja?*" Raynor glared at the bowling ball in his hand.

"It's one of them." Troy tilted his head. "You guys really don't have football in Norway?"

"It's not as, er, popular there." I guessed. "We prefer other things."

"Like skiing, right?" Troy's eyes lit up. "I bet you have wicked snow. Ours is so heavy here—it's like slogging through mud. I grew up back east, and it is mad different there. You know?"

"Mm-hmm." Janna didn't take her eyes off Raynor. He'd furrowed his brows while he walked *very deliber-*

ately toward the edge of the lane. He pulled his arm back as if he were moving in slow motion, then shifted it forward as he ever so gently released the ball.

It rolled straight into the gutter.

"Argh!" Raynor pounded his fist on his thigh. "This is impossible!"

"And that's the game." I gleefully tallied up our scores. "Ladies, we actually won this one. Thank you, Raynor."

"I just need to practice." Raynor stormed toward the counter, calling over his shoulder. "Who wants to go another round?"

"Not me." I stood, stretching my hands over my head. "I need a break. And possibly a new arm. That was grueling."

"Come on, shieldmaiden." Axel leaned in so only I could hear him. "I've seen you face tougher than that."

"*Ja*, well, the Cliffs of Conquest have nothing on bowling," I groaned. "I don't understand how something so small can cause so much pain."

"I can help with that." Axel's brow quirked. "I am *very* good with my hands."

Oh, are you now . . .

"Just kiss her, Andersson," Troy called out. "You talk about her enough—get it over with already."

My entire body went on lockdown. *Wait. What?*

Axel's eyes met mine, an unidentifiable emotion blazing from their emerald depths. My lips parted, and I drew a shaky breath as I slowly leaned away from the assassin. Disappointment washed over Axel's features.

146

Did he actually want to—was he seriously thinking—could he. . .

In the time it took me to *not* form a thought, Axel's arrogance had returned.

"It's not like that, man." Axel waved at Troy. "Ingrid's just a friend."

"Really." Troy arched one brow. "And all those things you say about her being so smart and so tough and so hot—"

"Don't you need another drink?" Axel shoved Troy toward the counter. The Alpha laughed all the way to the bar.

"I assume *hot* is the vernacular here for *strikingly beautiful?*" Janna blinked innocently.

Axel merely shrugged.

"I think that's enough conversation, thank you." I folded my arms.

"Whatever you say." Janna raised her hands in a shrug. "Brigga, you and I should go help Raynor. He seems pretty upset, and I'm afraid he's going to warrior out on that poor proprietor."

"Can't blame him, really." Brigga giggled. "He's terrible at bowling."

Truth.

"I'll go with you," Axel offered. "I've learned how to calm Raynor down over the years."

"I think you and Ingrid had better get over to the nightclub." Janna tilted her head at the room adjacent to the bowling alley. Inside, flashing lights pulsed to a thumping beat.

"We don't know how to dance to that." I jabbed my thumb in the direction of the music.

"You're smart. I'm sure you'll pick it up." Janna quirked her brows. "Besides, it's going to look suspicious if *none* of the exchange students are dancing."

Axel arched his brow. "How hard can it be?"

"Plenty hard," I muttered. But I reluctantly followed him toward the sound of the music.

Inside the club, a sea of students undulated beneath the flashing lights. The effect was disarming, each burst making it seem as if I was entering a different moment in time. Limbs jumped, rather than wove, into different positions, as the lights turned on and off in rhythmic succession.

"Well?" Axel gestured toward the dance floor. "Shall we?"

"I have no idea how to do . . . that." I stared as two of my sorority sisters swayed low to the ground, their legs in a stance that my current outfit wouldn't allow. "Is that how people dance here?"

"They're all doing it. Or that." Axel pointed surreptitiously to a couple engaged in what appeared to be a *very* intimate act. Only the fact that they were fully clothed kept me from covering my eyes with my hands.

"I'm not doing that, either," I said firmly.

"I'd never expect you to." Axel shook his head. "Unless you wanted to," he amended.

My fist connected with his shoulder.

"Ow! I was kidding!" He rubbed his arm. "Come on, shieldmaiden. Let's dance."

Axel reached out and wrapped his hand around mine. The heat from his fingertips sent a surge of energy coursing up my arm. My heart pounded as he tugged me forward, leading me onto the floor and pulling me lightly against him. I held my breath as our chests touched, and when I looked up, Axel was staring at me with that too-intense look that made my pulse quicken.

"Is this okay?" he asked quietly. His eyes didn't leave mine as I fought an internal battle.

Yes. No. I don't know.

"Axel! There you are! I've been looking for you *everywhere*."

The high-pitched voice I'd learned to loathe broke the spell. As I swung my head around to locate Lexi, my cheek brushed against Axel's chest. For the briefest of seconds, I let it linger there, inhaling the scent of forest and sweat and calm. How the Helheim did Axel smell like *calm*? And why had I noticed what he smelled like? He was Axel—the egotistical assassin whose overconfidence had nearly gotten us both killed.

Am I losing my mind?

"Oh. Ingrid." Lexi's disappointment dripped from her angular cheekbones. "You're here."

I placed my palms on Axel's chest and pushed away. "I was just leaving."

"Why?" Axel looked genuinely confused.

Because we're touching. And I like it.

"Because I, uh, need a drink," I blurted.

"I'll get you one." Axel moved closer, but I hurriedly stepped back.

"No, it's okay. I'm fine by myself."

"I know you are," Axel said easily. "But you don't have to be."

What exactly is he saying?

"Ingrid, be a doll and get me and Axel drinks, too." Lexi smiled sweetly. "I am absolutely parched. Aren't you, Axel?"

Axel glanced over at Lexi, who was practically spilling out of the scrap of fabric she wore as a top. Axel's lips parted and his eyes locked into place on their next target.

"Uh . . ." he mumbled.

Typical.

I turned on one heel, ignoring Lexi's self-satisfied smirk and Axel's complete lack of tact. The only thing I wanted to do was get away. I wasn't sure if that bus would take me home before the others, but there had to be some way to get to Kappa Mu . . . or anywhere that Axel Andersson *wasn't*.

I was halfway to the bar when a hand around my bicep pulled me back.

"Ingrid." Axel's voice was low. "Why are you running?"

"Just go be with Lexi." I couldn't keep the bitterness from my voice. "And stop pretending to be something you're not."

"What are you talking about?" Axel sounded genuinely confused.

"Oh, please. You're so transparent, Axel."

"Oh, am I?"

"Yes. You . . . what's the term here? You *hook up* with every girl you see. You live with no consequence to your actions, ever."

Axel's jaw twitched. "You think I live without consequences?"

"I know you do," I said. "And that's great for you—live your best life, and all of that. But when your choices start interfering with *my* life, and most specifically with my job, that doesn't work for me. I'm here on a mission, Axel. A mission that's of vital importance to my captain, my chieftains, and my clan. I can't afford the kind of distractions you seem to take on weekly."

"Again. What are you talking about?"

"Your endless stream of hookups."

"What the Helheim's a hookup?"

"Just go be with Lexi," I spat.

"Why would I want to do that?"

My hands balled into fists at my sides. "We all know the kind of guy you are."

"And what kind would that be?" he asked with deadly calm.

"You treat girls like they're expendable—you blow through them without a thought about what they want, or how being with you might affect them."

Axel crossed his arms. "For your information, I was always straightforward about what the girls I was with could expect from me. And I haven't been with anyone since I came back from Clan Bjorn."

"*Ja.* Right."

"It's true." Axel shrugged. "But that doesn't matter. It's clear that you evaluated my character long ago, and I came up lacking. I wish there was something I could do to change your opinion, but it seems you're a lot more closed-minded than you claim to be."

My gut clenched. No way was I letting him make me feel bad for a fact-based determination of his values.

"Axel!" Lexi's trill echoed through the bowling alley. "Are you coming back?"

Axel looked over his shoulder.

"Just go," I said. "I was leaving, anyway."

Axel's emerald eyes turned downward as he said, "You really can't stand me, can you?"

I faced the door and walked outside. I had no idea how I was getting back to the sorority, but I couldn't stay in that building one minute longer. If I did, I might do something I really regretted . . . like slug Axel in his perfect face.

Or kiss it.

The thought slammed into my brain with the force of a massive wave, and I shook my head to clear it. I did not want to kiss Axel. I did not want anything to do with Axel. The only thing I wanted was to do my job.

And then go the Helheim home.

CHAPTER 12

A S IT TURNED OUT, getting a ride wasn't going to prove too difficult. Kenzi pulled up in her car just after I stormed out of the bowling alley. She'd been logging extra hours at her work-study job, and couldn't get home in time to catch the bus. When she saw me standing at the curb with my hands balled into fists, she came over and gave me a hug.

"Bad night, huh?" she asked.

I shook my head. "You have no idea."

"I'm happy to drive you back to the house," she offered.

"Thanks. But I don't want you to miss the party." I glanced over my shoulder at the bowling alley of broken dreams.

Not broken dreams. Of independence. Of self-respect. Obviously.

"Meh." Kenzi shrugged. "Bowling's not really my

thing, and it gives me an excuse to bail without getting a demerit for not showing up."

"Ingrid! There you are!" Janna and Brigga burst through the building's front door. "My gods, what happened to you?"

"I'm ready to leave." I rubbed my arms to stave off the late fall chill. "Kenzi's going to give me a ride."

Janna glanced at Brigga. "We'll go with you," she said quickly. "Let me just go tell Raynor and Axel."

"Axel knows." I pulled my sweater tighter around me, doing my best to ignore Brigga's pitying look.

"I'm sorry, Ingrid," she said quietly.

"I'm not." I stepped closer to Kenzi. "Can we go now?"

"Of course." Kenzi pointed a small disc at her vehicle. "Car's unlocked now. Go ahead and wait inside. I'll just text Kayla so she knows not to hold the bus for us."

Kenzi grabbed her phone from her pocket, and I walked silently to the car. It only took me a minute to figure out that the rectangle on the side was a handle. Soon, I was tucked into a seat in the back, staring out the front window.

"Room for two more back here?" Janna asked quietly.

"You don't have to leave," I said. "I know you were having fun watching Raynor finally fail at a sport."

"Something tells me there are plenty of sports Raynor can fail at here." Brigga slid in next to me, while Janna took the seat beside her. "Their football is defi-

154

nitely more intense than he's up for. Not that he'd ever admit it."

"Mmm."

"Ingrid." Janna leaned over so she could look at me. "What happened in there?"

"Lexi's just . . ." I shrugged. "And Axel's . . . I mean . . ."

Brigga wrinkled her nose. "He didn't actually go for Lexi. Did he? Because that would be *beyond* disgusting."

"He probably will," I said. "That's just who he is."

"But—"

Janna was cut off by Kenzi's car door opening.

"What am I, your Uber driver?" She laughed. "Nobody wants to sit in front with me?"

My friends and I exchanged looks. We'd never ridden in a car—we didn't know the protocol.

"I'll come up," I said. I found the handle and opened my door, then moved around so I could sit in the front. "Sorry. We're just tired."

"Fair." Kenzi turned the key.

My entire body vibrated as the vehicle roared to life. "Is this thing safe?"

"It better be. It cost enough." Kenzi laughed as she pointed to the strap that hung near my shoulder. "Buckle up. We should be home in twenty, which will give me time to prep for tomorrow's field trip."

I glanced at Kenzi's torso, which had a fabric strap slipped across it. Taking my cue, I slid my own strap diagonally across my chest, then clicked the metal buckle into the small box on the seat. I glanced over my

155

shoulder, and subtly gestured for my friends to do the same. Then I turned around as Kenzi backed the car out of its spot.

"What's happening tomorrow?" I asked.

"My botany class has a field trip to a lake out near the desert." She looked to her left, then pulled onto the road. "It's home to some rare species of plants, and we're collecting a sample—with authorization, of course—to study."

Outside my window, cars and houses flew by. I knew everyone traveled this way here, but I couldn't help but shiver at the complete lack of control. It wasn't like I could jump out of this metal box if we were attacked by a bear, or a dragon, or whatever else posed a threat. I was strapped in, closed in, and totally stuck.

The future was beyond weird.

"What's your botany class like?" Janna asked Kenzi. "Do you study live samples?"

"We focus more on theory—why certain plants behave the way they do, optimal conditions for cross-pollination, all of that. But when there's something unique happening, like the lotus derivative that's currently blooming near Palm Desert, our teacher tries to incorporate it into her lessons."

My skin prickled. *That name* . . .

"Why did your teacher pick this one?" Brigga asked. "I'm sure there are a lot of blossoming flowers right now. You have a very mild climate."

"True," Kenzi agreed. "But apparently this flower

blooms underwater—which isn't unheard of, but it's rare in a desert. It only happens for one week every year, so we're going out there tomorrow morning. Our teacher has her scuba certification, so she's going to go down and pull up a sample for us. Pretty cool, right?"

My pulse quickened. "You're going to see a lotus derivative that blooms underwater?"

"Yeah." Kenzi merged across two lines of cars. "Why? Have you heard of it?"

"I think we read a story about it last week." I turned to the backseat. "Remember? The one with the lady in the lake? Her lake had something similar that bloomed in it."

Plus, the sample I pulled from our target contained residue from a mysterious aquatic plant . . .

Shieldmaidens didn't believe in coincidences.

"The lady in the lake, like from the King Arthur stories?" Kenzi grinned. "I'm pretty sure her lake was somewhere in England. But that would be a sweet mythological twist. Maybe there's a mysterious bridge that joins the two. Or a portal! Ha!"

Brigga paled. "Where did you say this lake was?"

"Out in the desert near Palm Springs—about two hours from school. Why? Do you want to come?"

"Can we?" I asked.

"Sure. I'm driving myself—I was planning to get in some shopping at the outlets while I was there. We can all head over together." Kenzi turned down a less-busy road, one framed by small buildings.

"That'd be really great," I said. "Thanks, Kenzi."

"Of course! We can talk energy on the drive there. I keep thinking of things I want to tell you outside of our chats, but I forget to write it down and . . . well, you know how it is." Kenzi turned right, and slowed her speed. We drove through house-lined streets for another few minutes before arriving on The Row.

"Home, sweet home," Kenzi said. She slid her car into one of the spaces behind the Kappa Mu house, and climbed out. "Sorry your night was a bust."

"Thanks for taking us home." I opened my door and followed her toward the rear entry. "It means a lot."

"Us yogis have to stick together." Kenzi grinned over her shoulder at me. "I've got some homework to catch up on, but I'll meet you downstairs tomorrow at five—no yoga class, unfortunately. The plant only blooms until eleven each morning, apparently because of lunar pull or something. Whatever it is, we have to be at the site no later than eight o'clock."

"We'll be here. Thanks again." I folded my hands together, and Kenzi mirrored my pose.

"Namaste, sister," she said as she slipped into the house.

I held the back door open for Janna and Brigga, then followed the two of them inside.

"We're meeting Kenzi downstairs at five," I relayed.

"You think this plant has something to do with . . . you know," Brigga whispered.

"No clue," I said honestly. "But Axel and I caught trace amounts of a water-based plant in the target's sample. It could have something to do with him."

"Or it could not." Janna bit down on her bottom lip. "I wish Freia had given us more information."

"I'll bet she wishes that, too." I walked slowly up the stairs. "We've already been here a week. I hope we're not working too slowly."

"We can only do what we can do," Janna reminded me. "But I'm glad we're expanding our search parameters. Odin willing, we turn something up tomorrow."

We have to. For all of our sakes.

CHAPTER 13

THE DRIVE TO PALM Desert was . . . enlightening. Not only did we get a crash course in twenty-first century high-speed travel, but we learned a *lot* about the lay of the land. It seemed that Los Angeles was comprised of centrally clustered high-rises from which spanned wide roads and *freeways*—a name that must have been given because people drove freely on them, without thought to safety or rules. Outside the city were slightly smaller towns, each of which still hosted more residents than existed in all of Valkyris-era Norway.

And every single one of them seemed to be on this particular freeway.

"Is this road always so slow?" I asked. We'd been sitting in an unmoving line of cars for the better part of ten minutes. Brigga and Janna had already fallen asleep. Bless their hearts.

"Pretty much." Kenzi reached for the cup she'd

placed in a holder, and took a hit. "That's why we left so early. Friday morning traffic is *the worst*."

Apparently.

"So this flower we're going to see," I said. "Besides being rare, is there anything else that's notable about it?"

"You mean, does it have any magical properties?" Kenzi teased. "Things that might summon the lady of the lake to produce the legendary sword of King Arthur?"

Heat flooded my neck. "No, that's silly."

And it was. The lady of the lake couldn't be real. But there *was* something about this plant . . .

"Is it?" Kenzi glanced at my snoring friends in her rear-facing mirror.

"Do *you* think it's silly?" I asked cautiously.

"On a logical level, maybe," Kenzi said. "But nothing's impossible. You know my family's big into energy, and the universal consciousness, and the power of intention to influence reality. So who am I to say this couldn't be somehow tied to another realm. I will say that my holistic friends are *really* excited about all of this."

"Why's that?" I asked.

"This flower we're going after today—it's supposed to possess an essence that's imbued with seriously strong energetic qualities."

"You've lost me." I craned my neck to see around the row of vehicles. They crept forward at a pace slower than I could walk.

"Every flower has an essence," Kenzi explained. "A fundamental property that, when distilled to a liquid, can transfer to whomever consumes it."

"Like . . . it will possess them?" I whispered.

"You can't be possessed by a flower." Kenzi rolled her eyes. "But you can use its properties to improve your emotional health, or expedite soul development."

Uh-huh.

"It turns out this particular flower—the one we're *hopefully* seeing today, if traffic ever lets up—is supposed to have the ability to transcend time."

What?

"Like, it can facilitate time travel?" I blurted.

"Time travel is a physical impossibility." Kenzi raised her cup to her lips. "At least, that's what my botany teacher would say. She's a woman of science."

"And you're a woman of . . ."

"The universe." Kenzi grinned.

"But how would that even work? How could a flower essence transport someone through time?"

"I have no idea." Kenzi slipped her cup back into the holder. "But if the illy flower even has minor physiological time-reversing effects—easing joint aches, or decreasing wrinkles—it could be a huge discovery."

The illy flower . . .

Huh.

"Of course." I stared out the window. If what Kenzi said was true—if this plant had the ability to manipulate time—then it could well be the source of our dark mage's magic. All we'd have to do was stake out the lake until he returned to collect a sample, then capture him and bring him in. It was the first tangible plan we'd had in a week. Too bad I couldn't tell my sleeping teammates about it.

Yet.

Three hours later, we finally arrived in Palm Desert. Kenzi slowed the car as we drove past a wooden sign labeled Latham Lake, and made our way down an old, dirt road. Dust kicked up outside my window, its particles forming thick, brown clouds around the glass. The haze obscured my view just enough that I didn't realize we'd reached the lake until Kenzi swore loudly.

She pulled up next to a massive bus. It looked just like the one that had taken us to the bowling alley the night before. "This can't be the site."

"Why not?" I opened my door, and stretched my legs as I stepped out of the car. Considering I'd done nothing but sit all morning, I was surprised I was so sore.

Still better than riding dragons, though.

Janna climbed out of the rear seat, and stood beside me. "Where's the lake?"

"It should be right there." Kenzi pointed to the massive hole in the ground. Around it stood two-dozen confused-looking students. "We've had plenty of rain; why would it be dried up?"

"Maybe she has some answers." I gestured to a

woman I could only assume was Kenzi's teacher. She looked to be a good thirty years older than the rest of us, with cropped grey hair and a pinched, angry expression.

"Good idea." Kenzi led us toward her teacher just as she began to address the gathered students.

"It appears I've taken you on a wild goose chase," the professor said curtly. "The colony illy flower, of which I took great pains to acquire a permit which allows me to extract *one member*, has been removed in its entirety from Latham Lake. Along with all residual flora. And water. This is an ecological impossibility, given the amount of rainfall Palm Desert has received over the past three weeks. Which leaves no doubt that this was a conscious act of destruction. One I can only hope ends with the arrest, and subsequent sentencing of its perpetrator."

Kenzi's jaw fell open. "Someone drained the lake? How?"

"Probably backed a tank truck up to it." The boy next to her shook his head. "Why would anyone destroy a protected region? It's a federal offense."

"Why would anyone remove *all* of a rare plant from one of its only known sources?" Kenzi frowned. "This doesn't make any sense."

I stepped backwards, and motioned for Janna and Brigga to follow. When we were a few feet away from the crowd, I leaned in and spoke in a whisper. "It must have been the dark mage. He drained the lake, and took all of the illy plants."

"Ingrid." Janna frowned. "I want to vilify him as much as the next shieldmaiden, but it seems highly unlikely we'd venture two hours from our base and land at the scene of a crime *he* committed."

"*Ja.* Besides, this seems outside his focus," Brigga added. "Why would he destroy a lake?"

"Because that's how he's traveling through time and creating his portals." I wrung my hands together. "He's using an extract from the flower that was supposed to be here."

"That makes no sense." Brigga shook her head. "Flowers can't do magic."

"This one can," I said. I quickly filled my teammates in on what Kenzi had told me in the car.

"You're saying flowers have essences," Brigga recapped doubtfully. "And if you distill them into liquids you can . . . absorb that essence into your body?"

"Apparently." I shrugged. "It sounded crazy to me, but Kenzi's more knowledgeable on current-day practices than we are. Maybe it's been this way all along, and people have only just figured it out. I don't know."

"Our seers use flowers," Janna reminded us. "We just never knew what for."

"Right." I rubbed the back of my neck. "Well, either way, it looks like our mage has collected more than enough of this illy to keep him going through multiple portal jumps. He's going to be even harder to track now."

"As if it wasn't rough enough already." Janna

groaned. "I guess we'd better get back to work. This was a dead end."

Except that . . . *oh. My. Gods.*

My stomach flipped as pins and needles shot through my body. *That's* why the flower sounded so familiar. How had I missed it?

"It wasn't a dead end. It's the answer we've been waiting for!" I glanced around to make sure nobody was listening, then turned my attention back to my friends. "Remember that spell we found in the library— the one to control all of mankind and the realms?"

"*Ja.*" Brigga frowned. "Why?"

"Some of the ingredients were crossed out, but two were clearly legible—quanta crystal, and illy bloom."

Brigga's lips formed a small *O*. "Do you think our target's trying to perform that spell?"

"I wouldn't rule it out," I said. "He may just want the plant for portal travel. Or . . ."

"Or he may want it for something worse." Janna swore. "This is bad."

"Really bad," I agreed. "But we finally have a lead on how to track him. If he's working on that spell, he's here to go after the ingredients. We have to get back to campus and find that list, map out all the regions that might contain the items, and then wait for him to show up and collect. So long as we maintain the element of surprise, we should be able to get him into custody."

"But first, the list," Janna confirmed. "We find it, memorize it, and—"

"And hope the target is nowhere near fulfilling it," Brigga added. "Otherwise . . ."

Brigga didn't have to finish her sentence. We all knew exactly what was at stake. But we had a workable plan.

Odin willing, we could pull it off.

CHAPTER 14

LATER THAT AFTERNOON, KENZI dropped us off at the Kappa Mu house. Since her field trip had been cut short, she'd decided to bail on shopping and head to an overnight retreat with her mom—twenty-four hours of silent meditation at a facility in the Hollywood Hills. While Kenzi went up to her room to pack, Janna, Brigga, and I ran to the house next door. Hopefully Raynor and Axel would be back from the class we'd skipped. We had a lot of work to, and we needed all hands on deck.

Even if I'd rather not see two of those hands for a long, *long* time.

"You're here. Good. We need to talk." Janna pushed past the pledge who'd answered the Alpha house door, and headed straight for the couches where Axel and Raynor sat. Each held a rectangular device in hand, and stared at a big screen.

"What are you doing?" Brigga trailed Janna into the living room.

"Playing a video game. No!" Axel groaned as Raynor leapt to his feet with a jubilant fist pump.

"Yes!" Raynor yelled. "Third time, Andersson. Pay up."

"Best five out of seven?" Axel offered.

"Hey!" I clapped my hands together. "Janna said we need to talk."

Axel and Raynor both looked at me as if I'd grown two heads.

"What's with you?" Raynor asked.

"We're here to work," I growled. "Remember?"

"I take it you learned something on your field travels?" Axel reluctantly lowered his device.

"It was a field trip," I corrected. "And yes. We did. Can we talk somewhere less . . ." My eyes roamed over the red cups, empty chip bags, and trio of couches holding half-sleeping males.

"Less gross?" Brigga offered, just as I said, "Less public."

"Sure." Axel walked out of the living room, and strode up the stairs. "Our room's quiet. Most of the guys are at the bar down the street."

"In the middle of the afternoon?" Janna trotted after him.

"It's Friday." Raynor shrugged. "Apparently the party starts at noon."

Huh.

I hung a right at the top of the stairs, and followed

Axel, Janna, and Raynor into what must have been the guys' room. It was sparse compared to ours—just two beds, each with unmatched linens, and one dresser.

And no attached bathroom.

"I know what you're thinking," Raynor said. "And no, it's definitely not Valkyris' castle."

"It's not even the shieldmaiden compound." I glanced around. "But it is better than camping."

Brigga was the last to enter. "Yikes," she muttered.

"Close the door," Janna instructed. "I don't want anyone overhearing."

Brigga pulled the door shut, and looked around the small room. "Where do we sit?"

"Anywhere, I guess." Raynor dropped onto one of the beds and patted the mattress next to him. "This spot's free."

I moved to claim it, but Brigga was too quick. She slid in beside Raynor, and beamed up at him. With a sigh, I took a seat on the opposite bed. Axel sat beside me, while Janna paced in front of the window.

"You all right, shieldmaiden?" Axel asked quietly.

"Never better. We have a lead." I nodded at Janna.

"You took off pretty fast last night. I just want to make sure you and I are—"

"Janna," I blurted. "Why don't you fill them in?"

"Gladly." Janna folded her hands together. "Earlier this morning, we discovered our target had drained a local—ish—lake, and extracted all of its plant life. We believe he did this for magical purposes, as the plant in question was the one mentioned in the spell we read last week—the one used to control mankind and—"

"And take over all the realms," Axel finished.

"Correct." Janna sounded surprised. "How did you remember?"

"I thought it was weird those ingredients were blacked out, so I brought the book home." Axel pointed to the stack beside his bed. "You think the dark mage messed with the text?"

"We know he collected all of the illy flower from the only nearby lake that housed it," I said. "And we know that flower is not just an ingredient in the takeover spell, but that it also assists in time and space travel. It's a portal creator—or, it can be if it's in the right hands."

"That's insane." Axel blew a low whistle. "A flower has magic?"

"Again, it needs the proper wielder," I reminded him. "But *ja*. Basically."

Axel groaned. "Great."

"We need to identify the remainder of the ingredients in that spell, then attempt to locate them before the dark mage does." Janna resumed pacing. "The illy flower was only in one location. Hopefully the rest are fairly isolated, as well. If we show up and the site's cleared, we'll know we missed our target on that one. But if the item's still there—"

"Then we wait for him to show up," I finished. "We ambush him, take him back to Freia, and preserve the world—both the one we're in, and the one we're from —from his control."

"Easy as that, huh?" Raynor crossed his arms behind his head, and leaned against his wall.

"Odin willing." Janna stopped in front of the dresser. "Axel, you said you had the book. Where is it?"

"Here." Axel leaned over to pick up the text. As he did, his arm brushed against my shin. I quickly tucked it under my other leg, and scooted toward the foot of the bed, *away* from Axel.

He straightened up, his eyes carrying a hint of hurt.

"Let's see the book," I blurted. "Maybe we can read through the back of the parchment?"

"Highly unlikely." Axel opened the text and lifted the page so it was perpendicular to the book. "He blacked out both sides. He wasn't messing around. I don't know why he didn't just take it with him—or destroy it."

"Maybe he couldn't." I lifted the book so I could study its cover. "See these dark spots around the edges? It looks like someone tried to burn it, but the fire couldn't have lasted long. There's only slight damage. Could the book have some kind of protection spell? And if so, does that mean we have an ally?"

"Gods, I hope so." Axel's fingers brushed against mine as he squinted at the cover.

I quickly withdrew my hand.

"Ally or no, we can't read the spell here." Brigga played with the edge of her braid. "Any chance there's another copy of the book somewhere?"

"Huh. I didn't think of that." Axel crossed the room and opened the bedroom door. "Hey," he called down the hallway. "Anybody home?"

"I thought they were all at a bar," Janna whispered.

Brigga just shrugged.

"Brooks. Hey." Axel stepped into the hall, the book still in his hand. "I'm looking for another copy of this. Do you know where I can find it? Would it be in the same library I found this, or one of the others, or—"

"Why don't you just look it up on the internet?" Brooks brushed his shaggy, blond hair out of his eyes.

"On the what-now?" Axel asked.

"The inter—oh, right. You guys are off the grid. Such a bold choice, man. Hold on." Brooks pulled his phone out of his pocket. "Okay, what's it called?"

"*Folklore of,* uh . . ." Axel glanced at the cover. "*Folklore of Medieval Times.*"

"I'm looking." Brooks tapped on the small device. "Okay, got it. Nope, that's the only copy in our school library system. But maybe on an outside source . . ." Brooks swiped at his screen, and tapped again.

"What's he doing?" Brigga whispered.

"They have an invisible network of information here," Raynor said quietly. "It's all inside their little boxes."

"How?" Brigga's eyes widened.

"No idea. It's some kind of massive disseminator system run entirely off of magic." Raynor pressed his lips together as Axel pinned him with a glare. "I mean, technology," he said in a quieter voice.

"Okay, I found it as an e-book on the library's website." Brooks looked up. "If you need the whole thing, I can loan you my reader. Or, if you just need a few pages, I'll print them out."

"We only need page two-hundred-and-twenty-seven." I spoke up. "Would you be able to print us that page?"

"Huh? Oh, hey." A slow smile spread across Brooks' face. "I didn't realize you guys had girls in there . . ."

"We're friends from back home," I said quickly. Emphasis on *friends*.

"Oh, really?" Interest sparked in Brooks' eyes. "Well, if you get bored hanging out with these guys, I'm right down the hall."

"Didn't you say you were going to print something out?" Axel's words came on a low growl.

"Yeah. Sure. Hold on." Brooks' eyes lingered on me one second longer than necessary. By the time he sauntered back down the hall, Axel's shoulders were uncharacteristically tense.

"That was easy," Raynor said. "We didn't even have to leave our room. This technology world is really quite convenient."

"Here you go, man." Brooks returned, paper in hand. "If you need anything else, let me know. I'm just working on a paper. *In my room.*"

The last bit was directed at me. I willed my cheeks to cool as I raised one hand in farewell. "Thank you."

"No worries, gorgeous." Brooks winked as he walked away.

"Down, Axel." Raynor laughed. "He's not going to hurt her."

"I never said he was," Axel countered. He unclenched his jaw as he carried the paper into the room. For a guy who'd more than likely hooked up with Lexi last night, he was in an awfully lousy mood.

Whatever.

I snatched the paper from Axel's hands. "Good! This copy's not redacted. But . . ."

"But what?" Brigga scooted to the edge of the bed.

"But I've never heard of half of these things." I shook my head. "Quanta crystal, moonstone, meteor rock, balboa bark?"

"Meteor rock is self-explanatory," Brigga said. "Pieces of space-matter have been landing on earth since the dawn of time."

I blinked at her.

"What? I'm a disseminator. I read things."

"Where did you read that?" I asked.

"In one of those publications our 'sisters' have in their sitting room," Brigga said. "*Scientific Quarterly*, I think?"

"Well, did *Scientific Quarterly* tell you where we might be able to find a meteor around here?"

"It did, as a matter of fact." Brigga lifted her chin. "The article said that a new sample had just been delivered to the Griffith Park Observatory. It was put on display because it's one of the largest space rocks ever procured."

My heart leapt into my throat. "That's it. That's

what he's going for. The largest space rock ever procured."

"How far away is that observatory?" Axel asked. "And how do we get there?"

"You guys are going to the Griffith Park thing?" Brooks popped his head around the corner. "Better hurry—the bus is leaving in ten minutes."

"What Griffith Park thing?" Axel shifted so he stood slightly in front of me.

It was rude, really.

"The sports program we run at Chavez Elementary." Brooks' brows furrowed together. "It's our fall philanthropy project. Chuck talked it up at Monday night dinner this week. If you go any two Fridays, you meet your philanthropy hours for the quarter."

"Ri-ght." Raynor clearly had no such recollection. "*Ja*, we're going. You say it's in Griffin Park?"

"Griffith Park," Brooks corrected. He tilted his head and met my gaze around Axel's body. "You ladies are more than welcome to join us. Our philanthropy is an after-school program for underserved kids. We take turns running activities on Fridays."

"That's really nice," Janna said. "I'll bet the kids appreciate it."

"Some of them do," Brooks said honestly. "Some can't stand us. They say we're a bunch of spoiled rich kids who don't know the first thing about inner-city life."

"Is there any truth to that?" I asked.

"Probably." Brooks laughed. "But I like it when they

call us out. Keeps it real, you know? Anyway, we'd love the extra hands. Looks like we're going to be short-staffed today."

"We'd be happy to go," I offered.

Axel's eyes narrowed. "For the kids?"

"Obviously for the kids." Did he think I was into his housemate? "Our people are all about serving others."

It was true. Valkyris stood for kindness, and honor, and the betterment of *all* of mankind.

Of course, we also stood for stopping the dark mage hell-bent on destroying and/or controlling the worlds. And this excursion would get us a free ride to exactly where we needed to go.

Score, us.

CHAPTER 15

C HAVEZ ELEMENTARY SCHOOL WAS a
sterile institution located a few miles down the
hill from the Griffith Park Observatory. Brooks
pointed out the multi-domed building as we crept
along the freeway, once again in mind-numbingly slow
traffic. It appeared that there was no good time of day
to drive in Los Angeles.

By the time we got to the school, class was already
out. The after-school program students gathered in a
massive room with shiny, wooden floors, a large open
stage, and nets that hung from metal circles set against
rectangular backboards. The kids were gathered
around a guy who looked to be a few years older than
us. He handed out ropes and balls, all the while going
over his expectations for the students.

"You're late!" A little boy with freckles across his
nose turned to glare at Brooks.

"I'm sorry." Brooks tousled the boy's hair. "Traffic was awful."

"You always say that!" another boy complained.

"That's because traffic is always awful." Brooks laughed. "You'll see when you're older."

"When I'm older, we'll fly bubble-powered jet packs!" A girl with pigtails beamed up at Axel. "They'll be environmentally friendly, and *way* faster than cars. Cuz, you know, there's no traffic in the sky."

Axel dropped to one knee. "I very much look forward to seeing your bubble pack."

"I drew a model! I'll show you!" The girl wrapped her fingers around Axel's arm and pulled him to his feet. He chuckled as he followed her to a table covered in art supplies.

"Where do you need us, Gary?" A group of Alphas approached the teacher. As they moved, the younger students jumped up and down to get their attention.

"They want to play basketball today," Gary answered. "Well, this group does. But some of them want to try archery, too—they just watched a cartoon about an Irish girl, and some bears, and—"

"I loved that movie." Brooks grinned at me. "The main girl looks like you, Norway. I never did catch your name."

"I'm Ingrid." I took his offered hand, and we shook. "And this is Janna, and Brigga."

"*Hei*," Janna said. Brigga offered a small wave.

"'Sup." Brooks nodded. "Come on. We can take the

archery group to the far end of the gym. Unless one of you prefers basketball?"

What's basketball?

"Archery's good," Janna said quickly. "Where are your arrows?"

"Oh, we don't use arrows." Brooks laughed. "Gary, are the foam darts still in the closet?"

"Yup." Gary pointed to the small room in the corner. Balls, hoops, and nets spilled from its nearly closed doors.

"Okay, archers, follow Miss Janna and Miss Brigga over there. Try not to get hit by any basketballs on your way." Brooks waved at the opposite end of the gym. "Ingrid, you and I can pull the archery sets. Come on."

"Sounds good." I dodged flying orange balls as I made my way across the room. Axel crouched by the art table, smiling at his young admirer. She spoke animatedly, gesturing to her paper and waving her arms as if she were flying. Axel laughed at something she said, then looked up and caught my eye. As our gazes locked, one corner of his mouth quirked up in a half-smile. A light fluttering suddenly nudged at my ribcage.

What the Helheim?

"Ingrid?" Brooks called. "You coming?"

Axel's smile morphed into a mutinous scowl.

"*Ja.*" I hurried after Brooks. Whatever was going on between him and Axel was not my issue. Ten kids were currently waiting on an archery lesson. And I wasn't about to disappoint them.

We gathered the materials, and brought them to the group.

"It's been a while since I've done this, so I may be a bit rusty," Brooks admitted.

"You just point and fire," a squeaky-voiced girl said loudly. "It's not like it's hard."

"Why don't you show me, Callie?" Brooks handed a bow and 'arrow'—a soft cylinder with a plastic circle on the end—to the girl. She took it in her tiny hands, and scrunched up her face.

"It's like this," Callie announced. She took aim at the circles painted on the wall, and let her arrow fly. The cup at the end hit the wall, sticking right at the center of the target. "Bullseye!"

"That was impressive," I praised. "You're a natural archer."

"I know," Callie said confidently. "I want to be a warrior, just like Merida."

I glanced at Janna. Who was Merida?

"Who's next?" Brooks asked.

"Me!" Another little girl stepped forward. She raised her bow, drew her arrow, and frowned as it shot straight onto the floor. "Dang it."

"That's okay—we all ground them sometimes." I helped the girl realign her bow. "What you need to do is lift your elbow . . . and don't release until you've *completed* your draw. Like this."

I guided her arms through the motions, keeping my fingers over hers until the string was fully taut. "Release it now," I coached.

She did as instructed. The arrow soared all the way to the wall.

"I hit it!" She turned around, a huge smile on her face. "I've never done that before!"

"You did great." I grinned back at her. "Try again—this time, without my help."

She picked up another arrow, and knocked her bow. When she hit the wall for the second time, she jumped up and down on her toes. "I can't believe it!"

"Way to go, Melanie. High five." Brooks held up one hand, and she slapped her palm against his.

"Why don't we break into groups?" Janna offered. "There are three targets—Brigga, Ingrid, and I can each take four students. Brooks, you can retrieve the arrows."

"Sounds good." Brooks nodded. "You heard Miss Janna—get into lines. Go."

While Brooks distributed the materials, I glanced across the gym to where Axel was now surrounded by three girls. He sat cross-legged on the floor, laughing while little hands wove braids into his hair. My pulse quickened as his eyes met mine again, and I couldn't help but smile at the sight of Valkyris' fiercest assassin getting his hair done by a trio of tiny admirers. Axel's dimple popped, and he shrugged as one of his stylists pinned a braid on the top of his head.

"Stay still!" the girl yelled, and Axel quickly dropped his shoulders and folded his hands. I couldn't hear what he said in response, but after a moment the girl looked over her shoulder and beamed at me. My cheeks heated as she turned back to Axel, cupped her hands to his ear, and leaned close to whisper something. When he looked up again, his eyes sparked with warmth.

And my pulse spiked anew.

"Look out!" Raynor's voice broke the spell.

I threw my arm up as an orange ball came flying at my head.

"Sorry. They bounce more than I expected," Raynor apologized.

"You never were our star athlete." I lobbed the ball back at him.

"Hey." Raynor bounced it with one hand, nearly tripping as he retreated to his game. "Maybe you have a point."

Laughter bubbled in my throat. "You know I do!"

"Hey, Ingrid?" Brooks appeared beside me. He dropped a pile of arrows at my feet, and met my eyes with a smile. "What are you up to later?"

Heading to the observatory to stake out a magical meteor and, hopefully, capture the dark mage I've been sent from the past to bring into custody.

"Just the usual," I said casually. "Why?"

"I was wondering if you might want to grab dinner." Brooks grinned. "Some of the guys are heading to a new club that just opened in Venice Beach, and there's a great Italian place not far from there. I figured we could eat, then go dancing."

My gaze slipped from Brooks' confident face, to the assassin sitting on the ground, his head now covered in braids *and* ribbons. Though Axel smiled at the girls, his jaw held a tension that hadn't been there before. He stared at Brooks as if he were a target—one he'd been given authorization to bring in cold.

Yikes.

"So?" Brooks pressed.

"Sorry, what?"

"Dinner? Dancing? What do you say?" Brooks' easy smile caught me off guard.

"Oh. Oh! Uh, sounds really fun," I said honestly. "But I've got plans with my friends tonight. Maybe another time."

Brooks followed my sight line to Axel. "Ah. I get it. You two are a thing."

"What? No. We are *definitely* not a thing. I just have stuff I have to do tonight. That's all."

"Uh-huh." Brooks sounded resigned. "Well, if you change your mind, you know where to find me."

He leveled Axel with a stare, then jogged across the room to retrieve the arrows from Janna's crew. Axel looked back at me from his yoga pose on the floor. His head tilted slightly, as if he wanted to ask what had happened between me and Brooks. I just shook my head and turned to my group as Janna moved to my side

"Did Brooks just ask you to go dancing?" She spoke into my ear.

"Mm-hmm."

"And did you just turn him down?" Janna pressed.

"*Ja.*"

"In Odin's name, why?" She placed her hand on her hip.

"We have a mission tonight, remember?"

"Oh, I remember." Janna stared at me. "But you could go out with him tomorrow. Or the next day. Unless you have another reason. Another, taller, *assassin-type* reason."

"Again. It's not like that," I muttered.

"Whatever you say," Janna said.

I shook my head as I picked up an arrow, and helped one of my charges line it up. As she shot, a high-pitched giggle from across the gym caught my attention. Axel's trio had found a dress-up box, and were crowning him with a sparkly tiara and scepter. He bowed regally to his adoring crowd, each of whom clapped in delight. He rose, and our eyes locked for the third time. A fresh wave of heat crept up my neck as he winked.

"Not like that, huh?" Janna's whisper made me jump.

"No. It's not like that." I drew my shoulders back and focused on the young archer in front of me. "It's not like that at all."

Is it?

CHAPTER 16

G ETTING TO THE OBSERVATORY was easier than I'd anticipated. When we finished at the school, we told Brooks we planned to meet some friends up the hill. He'd relayed this to the bus driver, who was happy to take a detour to drop us off. When the bus pulled away, I caught Brooks watching me from the window. He really was a nice guy. Maybe we could have been a thing in a different world.

Or a different time . . .

The observatory must have been a popular Friday night spot. Its entry was swarmed with well-dressed couples, apparently out for date night. Cars lined the parking area, and still more drove along the circular road, intermittently dropping off passengers. All in all, there must have been a hundred people just in the immediate area.

The crowd was plenty big enough to hide a dark mage.

"I'd suggest we split into teams." Janna pulled us over to a trail. We were removed enough from the crowd that she was able to draw her dagger from her backpack without attracting attention. "It's unfortunate that we aren't more sufficiently weaponed up, but we do what we can on short notice."

"This is a fact-finding mission," Brigga reminded her. "We're just determining the meteor's location, and assessing the probability of the target's attempted acquisition."

"The probability is one-hundred-percent, and if he hasn't come for it yet, he will soon." Axel pulled a thicker blade out of his bag. "Raynor, did you bring the throwing stars?"

"Right here." Raynor patted his pocket. He passed some silver discs to Axel.

"Excellent." Axel slipped the discs into his pocket, and dropped his bag behind the bush. "Leave your gear here—we can collect it later. If the target's nearby, we don't want our movement restricted."

"Fair enough." I slid my dagger into my belt, and covered it with my sweater.

"Janna, I agree we need to split up." Axel turned to my captain. "But let's locate the meteor first to see exactly what we're dealing with. Then we'll break into teams. Ingrid, you're with me. Brigga, you and Raynor stick with Janna."

"And what are we doing, exactly?" I pulled the trace from my backpack, and slipped it into my pocket. Then I dropped my bag into the bush beside Axel's.

"If he hasn't collected it yet, and I think that's a big *if* given he drained an entire lake recently, then he's going to come for it soon," Janna said. "Each team will scour the observatory—identify potential hiding spots, and optimal vantage points. And then we stake him out."

"Good thing I brought snacks." Brigga patted her own bag. "I can take this with me, right? I have a dagger, but . . ."

"You have two fighters with you. I think you'll be fine." I nodded at Brigga. "Okay. We move in. Be careful, everyone. We don't know what we're walking into."

"Can't be any worse than what we've seen," Brigga muttered. But she raised her chin and declared, "Let's move."

"You heard the disseminator." Raynor marched toward the observatory's entrance. The massive, white building was topped with three grey-black domes. Each was illuminated by upward facing lights, making the entire building seem to glow. As we approached, I caught sight of the vast expanse of city splayed out below. Night had fallen on Los Angeles, and the village now appeared as an enormous string of lights that stretched as far as my eye could see. Finding the dark mage here would be like searching for a needle in a haystack. The only thing we had going for us was the knowledge of what he was after.

Odin willing, he hadn't come for it yet.

We walked inside, past a bulbous, swinging pendulum, and toward a wall that held a direction card.

"The observatory is over there." I pointed. "Planetarium is this way. And the museum is here. I'm guessing rocks and minerals are kept in the museum?"

"Most likely," Brigga confirmed. She followed the arrow to the left, and the four of us marched after her. We rounded a corner, and sucked in a collective breath.

"Found it," Axel whispered.

"Whoa. Is that . . ." I walked slowly around the enormous rock. It was easily the size of a car, with mottled grey and black holes cobbled across its uneven surface. "How'd they even get it in here?"

"Oh, we have a service door specifically for large-scale items." A cheerful, white-haired woman wearing a tag that said *Dottie* approached from my right. "Though this particular specimen broke on impact, and has actually been reassembled at four points. See that crack right there?"

I followed her finger to a barely visible seam in the meteor. "I do now."

"Well, that's one of our seals. There are three more on the opposite side." Dottie smiled. "We were so excited to get this specimen. We thought it might go to one of the national museums in Washington first, but our little observatory won the rights. For this month, anyway. Then it moves on to the next lucky site."

"How long has it been here?" Brigga walked over to Dottie.

"About a week. And I must say, it's attracted quite a bit of interest—especially from young people!" Dottie clapped her hands together. "Why, just an hour ago, a

fellow about your age was asking me about its properties. Which part of the desert it touched down in,
whether any elements would have transferred into its
core. I had to get one of our scientists from the lab—
I'm just a docent, and his questions were much too
complicated for me. But it was such a joy to see his
enthusiasm. He'd even dressed the part, though his
scientist robe was a bit off—black, and more of a cape
than a lab coat. Still, I did appreciate the effort. Most
people your age would rather be playing video games,
and to see such an interest in science—"

"Um, Dottie?" I asked. "This young man—what did
he look like?"

"Well, he wasn't tall—I remember because his outfit
seemed far too big for him. And he was quite out of
shape, bless his heart. He could do with a hike—we
have the loveliest trails, and even host stargazing hikes
at night. Shoot, I should have told him about those. He
seemed like he didn't have many friends. Maybe he
could have met some nice boys and girls and—"

"Was his hair black?" I pressed. "Kind of stringy, and
shoulder-length?"

Dottie pursed her lips. "I do believe it was. Why? Do
you know him? Oh, good. He *does* have some friends.
It's so hard these days, with the computers and social
media and all of those *devices* to keep you young people
from truly connecting with one another. It's a shame,
really, that progress has made you regress socially.
Why, when my Richard and I were young, we—"

"Dottie, I'm so sorry." I placed my hand on the

woman's arm. "We have to go. Thank you for talking with us. You've been incredibly helpful."

"I'm so glad to hear it. It's always a delight to see youth with a passion for science!" Dottie clasped my hands between hers. "Do come again, won't you? Next weekend is the full-moon night hike. I think you'd get a kick out of our scientist's talks on—"

"We'll try to make it!" I slipped away, and motioned for my team to follow. "Thank you, Dottie."

"Goodbye!" she called after us.

I strode purposefully toward the far end of the room. I ducked into a corridor, and waited until Janna, Brigga, Axel, and Raynor joined me.

"She was talking about him, wasn't she?" Axel asked. "Our target was here an hour ago."

"He fits the description," I confirmed. "Short. Doughy. Greasy black hair."

Axel glanced over his shoulder. "The question is, where is he now? And how do we draw him out?"

"I've got the trace." I patted my pocket. "If he's within a few miles, I can release it and it will lead us to him. But if we're wrong . . ."

"We'll have blown our one chance at a confirmed track." Janna shook her head. "I don't know. I think maybe we should—oh!" She slammed into the wall as the room jolted sideways. "What's happening?"

I stumbled backward, the ground trembling beneath me. A loud crack rang from the meteor's room, and the walls around us wobbled.

"What the Helheim?" Axel drew his dagger.

"It's not an attack. It's an earthquake." Brigga braced herself against the wall. "I read about them in—"

"Look out!" I jumped forward, pushing Janna out of the way as a mounted crystal toppled from its perch. The massive gem shattered into shards, splintering the floor and sending a burst of light through the corridor.

"That's no earthquake." Axel threw himself in front of me. He raised his dagger and quickly scanned the corridor. I wasted no time in drawing my own blade.

"You think it's him?" I spun so my back was to Axel. This way, we had a full view of the area. "If the dark mage is here, we have to pull the trace. Janna, cover me."

Janna pulled out her blade and slid into my place behind Axel. Raynor and Brigga each pulled out their own weapons as I tugged the trace from my pocket. I quickly unscrewed the lid and held the tube up high. A gold, sparkling mist rose from the container. It swirled overhead three times before snaking along the corridor and angling toward the main room.

"Follow it," I ordered. "And don't step on those crystals."

"Wasn't planning on it," Raynor muttered. He led the charge along the hallway. Axel was close on his heels.

"Stay with us." I ran behind Brigga. "We'll cover you."

Brigga exhaled. "I am perfectly capable of taking care of my—oh, gods."

I careened around the corner and promptly sucked

in a breath of my own. The meteor, which had been one fused continuous piece moments ago, lay in quarters on the floor. It emitted low pulses of light—tiny waves that rose from the rock and wafted toward the high ceiling. Either it was putting out some kind of a charge, or it was . . . was it about to explode?

"We have to clear the room," I shouted. My head whipped from side to side as I searched for the docent who'd helped us earlier. I found her standing in a doorframe, her hands and feet braced in each corner.

"Dottie!" I screamed. "You have to get out of here! Everybody has to get out of here! Now!"

"The tremors will pass," Dottie called back. "We were due for a little quake."

"This is not a little quake." Brigga herded the half-dozen people still in the room toward the exit. "You all need to evacuate. Get as far from the building as you can. This meteor is unstable."

"Nonsense. It's merely reacting to the seismic shift that's typical of—"

"Dottie, I mean no disrespect. But get out. Now." Axel picked the old woman up and carried her toward the museum's main room. "All the way outside. We'll handle things in here."

"Now, young man," she protested loudly. "If there's a risk, observatory protocol dictates—"

Her voice faded as Axel forcibly removed her from the premises.

"Where'd the trace go?" My eyes sought out the

golden trail. It wove around the meteor, dipped low, then snaked toward the wall.

"Why does it drop down over here?" Janna walked carefully across the still trembling ground. She knelt beside the broken meteor, and promptly swore. "There's a piece missing."

"Are you sure?" I ran over to my captain, and examined the rock at her feet. Not only did it have a bowling ball-sized hole, but a circle of black residue was pooled where the piece should have been.

"Trace is going that way." Brigga pointed to the golden trail in the air.

"On it." Raynor charged after the dust. It had stopped at a door marked *Emergency Exit*. Raynor wrenched the door open. The blare of an alarm filled the room, its volume nearly shattering my eardrums. But my focus remained on the dust, which snaked through the newly opened door and headed into the night.

"Go," I barked. Without waiting for my friends, I raced outside. A chill had crept over Los Angeles, but I couldn't tell if the goose bumps covering my arms were from the cold or from the realization that we were about to catch our perpetrator. The target was close.

And this time, he wouldn't get away.

CHAPTER 17

MY LEGS BURNED AS I raced through the woodlands behind the observatory. The trace had taken us across the entry lawn, along a hiking path, and on a trek that felt miles deep into the tree-lined hills. The Hollywood sign stretched below us, all but its now-missing 'D' visible in the moonlight. We had to be getting closer to the mage. The trace kept moving forward, guiding us through brush and dirt and—

"Ingrid, get down!" Axel's throaty cry stopped me. I pressed my cheek to the ground as a blast of light shot through the exact spot on which I'd just stood. I rolled quickly onto my back, cataloguing the impact site and likely place of origin. The tree behind me smoldered, its bark emitting a thick, black smoke. While to my right . . .

It's him.

I arched my back and leapt onto my feet, squaring my shoulders as I raised my dagger. The dark mage

195

stood poised atop a boulder. His black cape billowed behind him, and his saggy jowls trembled as he threw his head back and roared.

"Move any closer and I'll destroy you!" he bellowed.

"You'll have to hit me first." I dropped to a fighting stance, and waited for the mage's blow. He lobbed a light beam, which I parried easily with my blade. The beam landed hard in the dirt, sending a sparking dust-ball flying into a nearby bush.

"Janna, look out!" Raynor yelled at my captain. She spun away from the flaming bush, and charged our target.

The mage raised one hand, and flicked his fingers. A force field shot from his palm, its wavy blue-grey light spiraling through the air like a disc. It struck Janna in the chest and she doubled over, cringing as her knees cracked against the ground.

"Janna!" I screamed.

The mage turned to me, drawing his fingers to his palm in what was likely to be a repeat attack. Nearby, Axel had slipped one of the discs from his pocket. When he arched one brow, I nodded. Without giving the mage time to react, I bent my knees and leapt for the side of the trail. I sprinted in a serpentine pattern, dodging and weaving, and making it impossible for my attacker to get a clear shot. He threw a half-dozen force fields, but none connected . . . and none slowed my sprint. I'd halved the distance between us, careful to ensure the mage's attention remained fully focused on me, when Axel flicked his wrist. The silver throwing star slipped easily from his palm, rocketing toward its target with the speed of a furious dragon. The mage let out an enraged roar. Axel's weapon had hit its mark.

"That's for destroying a seriously rare meteor," I shouted as I ran closer.

"I didn't destroy it." The mage flicked another force field.

This time, I barely managed to duck out of its way.

"I released its resonance. It's fully functional now, in vibrational alignment with—" He let out a garbled howl as Axel's second disc hit him square in his throat.

"With what?" I called. "What are you aligning that meteor with?"

The mage ripped the disc from his neck and flung it at Raynor. My friend swatted it away with his blade, then flung his own star in return.

"We can play this game," Raynor growled. He pulled two more stars, firing on the target in rapid succession.

Blood streamed from the mage's throat as he used one hand to deflect Raynor's discs. Beams shot from his fingertips, redirecting the weapons in an energetic surge. They reversed course, forging a path straight for Brigga. Right before they reached her, Raynor threw himself in her path. He swatted one disc away with his dagger, but the second lodged securely in his forearm. His shout echoed through the hilltops.

We were seriously outmaneuvered.

The mage set Axel in his sights, raising both hands and crooking his fingers inward. I lowered my dagger so it aligned with the target's gut, and pumped my legs harder as I ran. I wasn't going to let that monster use his magic again . . . and I sure as Helheim wasn't about to let him hurt Axel.

With a cry, I launched myself off my toes, leaping forward in a trajectory that should have put me on a course to impale our attacker. But as I soared through the air, the mage shifted his focus from Axel to me. He swiped his fingers to one side, throwing me easily to the ground and destroying any hope I had of gaining the upper hand. Pain shot from my heels up my legs, tiny shards piercing my bones in an unrelenting rhythm. I rolled onto my back, clutching my knees to my chest and trying not to think about the burning sensations in my shins.

Focus, Ingrid. How are you going to get your team out of this?

While I assessed my injuries, the mage turned to Axel. He shot a pulse from his fingertips, filling the air with a greyish-black light. A crack pierced the night as the light struck Axel. His spine bent back, and his still-braided hair stood on its end as the charge worked its way through his body. His face contorted while his torso froze in clear agony. If the mage hadn't had a magical hold on him, I doubted he'd have been able to stay upright.

Our assailant sent another charge at Axel, and I rolled onto my stomach. I tried to climb to my feet, but my right leg buckled beneath the weight. With a groan, I limped slowly toward the mage. He was so focused on Axel, he didn't appear to notice me coming. I waved my hand at my side, sending a silent signal to the now-standing Janna. Her own hand balled into a fist—she was telling me to hold. *Hold? While Axel's getting cooked alive?* I shook my head, but Janna dropped to her stomach and shimmied through the bushes. She was going for the element of surprise.

Which meant I'd have to be the bait.

Raynor was still down, and Brigga was trying to remove the disc from his arm. We were outpowered, outwitted, and running out of time. But I wasn't about to give up.

Shieldmaidens never backed down.

I drew a shaky breath and hopped forward. My plan was to get as close to the target as I could, and hopefully draw at least some blood before Janna took him out. If I could keep him distracted, maybe Janna could get near enough to cut his ankles. Even a top-level mage couldn't stop an arterial bleed-out.

I hope.

The mage sent a fresh charge through our assassin, and Axel threw his head back, howling in pain. I charged forward without thinking. My knee popped with each step, but I pushed through the gut-churning pain. When I was ten feet away, I drew my arm and used my good leg to launch myself at the monster hurting my friend. The mage turned his head, his eyes widening as I swung my dagger. For the second time that night he flicked his fingers at me, sending me flying into the dirt. Pain exploded across the back of my head as I collided with a boulder . . . or a bush. Or maybe it was Raynor. It was impossible to tell what was happening with stars swimming in front of my half-closed eyes.

I rolled my head to the side, pressing my cheek against something rough while Janna crept up behind the mage. She jammed her blade through his back, twisting it with a ferocity that left no doubt she'd struck to kill. The mage's arms dropped and Axel fell hard. His limbs twitched as the dark magic worked its way out of his body. A flash pulled my attention to our target, who was screaming in an ancient-sounding language. Panic swept over me as a bubble of light enveloped the mage. He was casting a spell! If Janna didn't stop him he'd—

POP!

He disappeared in a flash of silver light. Janna tumbled forward as he vanished, her palm still on the handle of her now-bloodied dagger. The mage was gone. Our team had failed. And our mission . . .

How were we supposed to catch him now?

"Status report?" Janna barked.

"Immobile, but alive," I replied.

"In a *dritt*-ton of pain, but alive," Raynor called.

"Covered in Raynor's blood and completely nauseous but also alive," Brigga said.

"Axel?" Janna called.

Silence.

"Axel?" Janna tried again.

Oh, gods.

"Axel?" I shouted. "Are you all right?"

Nothing.

My stomach dropped, and cold sweat broke out across my forehead. Seconds felt like years as I pushed myself up on my palms and dragged one leg in front of me. The sudden surge of pain made it clear that walking was out of the question, so I dropped to my backside and scooted across the dirt. As I struggled, Janna rushed to Axel. She lifted his wrist and pressed two fingers to its underside.

"Is he . . ." I couldn't bring myself to finish.

"He has a heartbeat," Janna confirmed.

My torso folded in on itself. "Oh, thank gods."

"But he's in shock. We need to keep him warm." Janna looked around, presumably for a jacket. She wasn't going to find one—we'd left our bags back at the observatory.

"Here." I ripped my sweater over my head, and scooted the rest of the way to Axel. He was pale as snow, with a faint sheen of sweat lining his brow. His fingertips still twitched, and his overall appearance was decidedly *not good*.

Please, gods, let him be okay.

"This should help." I tucked the fabric around Axel's shoulders. His chest quivered as I wrapped the sleeves beneath his arms. Whether his body was reacting to cold or shock or still processing the massive bolts of energy that had been fired into him, I couldn't tell. Axel was in trouble.

And I'd do everything in my power to help him.

Maybe it was because he'd helped free me from

Clan Bjorn. Or because he'd taught me how to fight—and given me the freedom to know I could always take care of myself, no matter what came at me in the future. Maybe it was that he'd offered me the gift of independence—never tried to put me in a box or set limits on what I could achieve. Or maybe it was because he just looked so helpless lying flat out, with all of those braids and ribbons still in his hair. But in that moment, I knew without a shred of doubt that Axel Andersson had worked his way into my heart.

And I wasn't sure that I wanted him out.

"You'll be okay, Axel." I rubbed my hands along his forearms. "Janna, can you elevate his legs? Maybe pull over some of those larger rocks, and prop them up on those."

"Absolutely." Janna located two small boulders, and dragged them toward Axel. She lifted his legs so his feet were above his heart. "This good?"

"*Ja*," I said. "If he doesn't come to in a minute, we'll check his pulse again and consider administering resusci—oh, thank gods! You're awake! Raynor, Brigga, Axel's awake!"

Relief blossomed in my chest as Axel's eyes blinked open. He looked around in confusion as he tried to sit up.

"Stay down," I ordered. "You've had a major trauma."

"Feels like it," he groaned. "My chest is on fire."

"You got hit with some massive light beams," I told

him. "The target had you in a lock for a solid minute—maybe two."

"Did we catch him?" Axel croaked.

"No. Janna nearly had him, but he disappeared again. But that's not my concern right now. Are you dizzy?"

"Extremely," Axel confirmed.

"I don't blame you." Raynor limped slowly to my side, with Brigga supporting him on her shoulder. "That looked awful. Sorry he got to you, man."

"Thanks." Axel winced as he pushed himself up on one elbow.

"I said to stay down," I admonished.

"I'm not great at taking directions." Axel shrugged. "You should know that by now."

"I'm just glad you're okay. I thought for a minute you were . . ." I bit on my bottom lip.

"Takes more than a dark mage to get rid of me, shieldmaiden." Axel reached up and tucked a curl behind my ear. "But I'm glad to know you care."

"I never said that," I objected.

"And I'll never ask you to," Axel promised.

A flood of conflicted butterflies took flight behind my ribcage as Axel pushed himself to a seated position. One corner of his mouth tugged upward as he pulled my sweater from his shoulders and tucked it back around mine. Then he turned his attention to our team. "What's our plan now?"

"I don't honestly know. We used our one trace, so we don't have any magical help finding our mage. Plus, we know that even if we do locate him, we can literally stab him in the back and he can still disappear just like that." I snapped my fingers with a sigh.

"But we also have a list of items he needs for his spell," Janna reminded me. "If we can source the ones he hasn't found, we might be able to stake him out again."

"And do what?" I asked. "You had a dagger in his spine and he still got away."

"We have an idea," Brigga offered.

Three heads turned toward her and Raynor.

"We saw something while Axel was in his . . . state," Brigga said quietly. "The mage's beams illuminated what looked like a camp, about fifty yards down the hill. I didn't think anything of it, except that our target kept looking in that direction. I wonder if, maybe, we stumbled onto his home base."

My breath caught. "You think he's been living in these hills?"

"It would explain why the trace led us here," Raynor said. "We need to check out that campsite. There may be intel there that we can use."

"Can you walk fifty yards?" I sized Raynor up. Brigga appeared to be supporting a good percentage of his body weight.

"Can *you*?" he countered.

I tentatively flexed my leg. My knee popped, sending a surge of fireballs coursing up my leg.

"Don't think so." I winced.

Axel moved closer. "Can I touch it?"

"Not if you don't have to," I said.

"We undergo a fair amount of medical training in the assassin's program," he reminded me. "I won't do anything without your permission, but I do think I can help alleviate your discomfort."

"Fine." I bit the inside of my cheek. "Just be fast."

"Pain's eighty percent mental. You know that." Axel gently slid his hands along my thigh. He applied slight pressure to the top and bottom of my knee, then did the same on either side of the joint. I dug my fingertips into the dirt as the pressure led to pain.

"It may be mental, but that does *not* feel good," I relayed.

"It's dislocated." Axel released my leg, and reached over to hold my hand. "I can pop it back in, but it is going to hurt. A lot."

"I thought pain was eighty percent mental," I said.

"*Ja.* Well, this is going to push those limits." He squeezed my hand. "Are you okay with that?"

"No. But it's not like we have a ton of options." I drew a shaky breath, and released Axel's hand. "Just do it."

Axel nodded. He leaned in until his forehead touched mine. This close, I picked up on the heady blend of forest and calm that was so uniquely Axel. How did I know his scent? And more importantly, why did I care when he was about to rip my leg out of its socket, or maybe push it back into its socket, and—

"Just keep your eyes on me," Axel said calmly.

My gods, his breath smelled amazing. Like the

freshly blooming mint in the Valkyris gardens after a rainfall.

Why am I noticing how Axel smells?

"Okay, I'm going to apply some pressure. Then, once I'm sure you're in alignment, I'll make the tweak."

"You don't have to narrate," I said breathlessly. "I'd rather not know what's coming."

"Fair enough." Axel's eyes, just inches from mine, crinkled at the corners. "Well, then I should probably tell you that the braids those girls put in my hair gave me a massive headache. Or maybe all the tension in my scalp is a result of the light beams that were shot into it. I'm not entirely—"

"Argh!" Agony ripped from my knee all the way through my body. Every fiber of my being registered pain on a level I'd never experienced before. My vision blurred, and I swayed unsteadily as darkness overtook the outside of my periphery. Axel's hands shifted from my knee to my shoulders. He steadied me as I leaned to one side, intent on curling into a tight ball, and possibly dying.

"Good job, shieldmaiden," he whispered into my ear. "It's over."

I swore at him. "That was *not fun.*"

"I told you it wouldn't be," he said quietly. "But you did it. You always do."

His lips brushed against my cheek as he pulled away. Was that a kiss? Or just coincidence?

Why was I reading so much into every little thing?

"I'll stay with Ingrid if the three of you want to

check out the site." Axel turned to the rest of our team. "I doubt she'll be able to walk for a bit."

"I want to see it," I objected. "I'll hop if I have to."

"You sure?" Janna looked at me with concern. "You're green."

"I'm tough," I corrected. "And I'm going."

Axel's eyes moved up and down my still-hunched body. "I'll carry you," he decided.

"I can walk." I tried to stand . . . and promptly found myself back on the ground. Raising my chin, I said proudly, "I accept your offer."

Axel helped me onto one foot. Then he swept me up, hooking one forearm behind my thighs and resting the other against the small of my back. "Hold onto me," he coached, and I awkwardly wrapped my arms around his neck. A wave of dizziness washed over me, and I rested my cheek on Axel's chest as I fought to regain my equilibrium.

"You okay?" His chin moved against my forehead.

"*Ja.* Just a head rush."

"Relocating your knee can do that." He pulled back so he could meet my gaze. "Let me know if you want me to put you down."

"What I want is to see the target's base camp. Move it, Andersson."

Axel's chest rumbled with laughter. "You heard the shieldmaiden. Janna, you taking point?"

"Always." Janna led us down the hill. We made quite the travel party, with Raynor leaning heavily on Brigga, and Axel carrying me in his ridiculously thick arms.

No, not thick arms. Normal, unimpressive—

Oh, let it go. They're spectacular arms.

They really were.

In the five minutes it took us to walk down the hill, Axel asked if I was hurting ten times. And when we rounded the final corner, he shifted so I'd see the base camp at the same time he did. The camp didn't look like much—it could easily have been an abandoned tent, or a wanderer's temporary rest spot. But it emitted the sweet, fruity scent of a flower . . . probably a lotus flower, though I'd never smelled one before. And the entire area was swathed in the thin, black film of dark magic.

"This is definitely his base," Axel deduced. He walked along the perimeter, careful not to get too near the residue. "Look, he even left the fire burning. We must have caught him off guard."

Janna picked up a pitcher, and poured its contents over the fire. The flames sizzled as they went out, and she kicked dust over the embers to ensure they were extinguished. The last thing we needed was to draw more attention to ourselves by setting the hills on fire. That would earn us an ethics violation, for sure.

Snort.

"Look in there." I pointed to the inside of the makeshift tent. It was no more than a trio of tarps strung up against a tree, but it contained a veritable trove of treasures. A massive pot, dried meats, rolls of what looked to be moldy bread, a bedroll, and . . . "Is that a map?"

"Janna, cover me. I'm moving in." Axel waited for Janna's confirmation. When my captain had drawn her dagger, Axel stepped carefully into the tent, still carrying me in his arms. I bit my lip, wondering whether we'd be sucked into another dimension or transported through an invisible portal, but nothing happened. Cool breath brushed against my forehead as Axel exhaled. I pointed at the map pinned to the side of the mage's tree-wall.

"That thing, right there. What does it say?"

Axel walked forward. He shifted me to one arm so he could pluck the map from its resting spot, then carried us both to the camp's perimeter. He handed the map to Janna, who spread it on a tree stump. We all gathered around.

"I think it's a series of convergence sites. See how he's created circles across certain latitudes?" Axel carefully set me down on one foot. He kept one arm firmly around my waist, ensuring I didn't have to put any weight on my still-throbbing knee. "The ocean's right here, with the Hollywood Hills to the east and to the south . . . what's Latham Lake?"

"The location he pulled the illy flower from—the plant he's using to jump time." I studied the map. "What do you mean by convergence sites?"

"Well, my cartography's not the greatest, but I do remember learning to chart stars and planetary shifts. We do it so we understand tidal changes on seafaring voyages," Axel explained.

"And?" Brigga asked.

"And it looks like he's mapped out not only locations of items—probably the ones from his spell list—but also of energy." Axel pointed. "These circles seem to indicate an alignment of celestial bodies that will funnel power directly into this spot."

I narrowed my eyes at the writing by Axel's finger. "San Diego? Why?"

"No idea." He shook his head. "Maybe it's going to receive some kind of cosmic surge he can draw from, or maybe there's going to be another meteor crash that will bring him an element he needs."

"It's so thorough." Raynor scanned the parchment. "Illy flowers, quanta crystals, meteor rocks. Everything from the list is mapped out by location. There's even one on the college's campus. No name, but a drawing . . ."

We all leaned forward to study the rudimentary sketch. It seemed to be a blade—one held in a handle covered in runic writing and gemstones.

"Oh my gods," I whispered. "That's Freia's dagger."

Janna turned to me with wide eyes. "He's after our dagger?"

"It appears so," Axel said grimly.

"He saw it the night he destroyed the statue. He looked relieved." I remembered. "We knew this was a possibility."

"Then why didn't he take it then?" Brigga asked. "If it's on his list, surely he wouldn't just let it get away."

"He probably figured he'd have another opportunity," Janna said grimly. "And he would have, tonight, if he hadn't been distracted by trying to kill Axel."

"He could have taken it tonight if he'd wanted to," I corrected. "All he had to do was turn those light beams on me and I'd have been frozen instead of Axel. Maybe it's a sequencing issue—maybe he doesn't want it until he's collected everything else."

"But why does he need this stuff at all?" Brigga asked. "Surely, a dark mage can 'control mankind and all the realms' without needing to rely on some spell."

"Because." Raynor limped slowly toward the tent. "He's not just looking to *control* the realms. He's looking to recreate them."

Goose bumps broke out across my arms. "What are you talking about?"

"This." Raynor picked up a leather-bound book that lay open on the bedroll. He carried it to the tree stump, and set it down on top of the map. "The mage has a breakdown . . . of what he'll need to do to erase Valkyris from existence."

"That's not possible," Janna said.

"It is if he completes the spell." Raynor slid his finger along the yellowed parchment, and read aloud. "Collect ingredients. Enact control. Port to five-years pre-Valkyris founding. And . . ."

"Murder Freia," I whispered. "No. No, that can't be."

"Her dagger is on his collection list," Raynor pointed to a column on the opposite page. "If he has possession of it, my mother can never establish our

island. And if he kills her before she meets my father . .
"

Oh. My. Gods.

Axel turned to me. Our eyes met in a worried stare. If Freia never met Halvar, Raynor and his brother wouldn't be born. Valkyris wouldn't exist, and its shieldmaidens would be nothing more than an idealized dream. None of us would have ever come together. And the world we were working to build back home—one of honor, and valor, and virtue, and kindness . . . it would die before it had even begun.

I leaned heavily on Axel as the reality of our task draped like wet wool across my shoulders.

We had to stop the target. Everything we had ever known depended on it.

CHAPTER 18

I T WAS A SLOW walk back to the observatory. Not only were half of us in immeasurable pain, but the enormity of our situation had finally hit home. This wasn't just a mission—a test to prove to Freia—and myself—that I was good enough to be on the Shield-maiden Squadron. This was a matter of life and death, of existence or . . . nothingness.

No pressure.

We retrieved our backpacks from the bushes and limped into the observatory parking lot. Once there, we realized that we had no way to get home. We'd taken the Alpha's bus here, but none of us knew how to utilize the city bus system to get back. The gods must have taken pity on us, because Morgan pulled into to the lot while we were staring at the stars, wondering how long it would take to hobble back to campus. She'd been planning to catch the planetarium show with a friend, but she took one look at us and offered to take us home.

"We don't want to ruin your night," I objected. "We can wait until your show's over."

"It's the same show every weekend," she said drily. "I'll text my friend and cancel. Jeez, you all look like you're about to pass out. What kind of hike did you take?"

Hike. Sure.

"A rough one," Axel answered. "Very high difficulty rating."

"Did you run into a mountain lion?" Morgan gaze moved from my limp to Raynor's bloodied arm to Axel's singed shirt.

"We fell," I lied. "I hit a patch of mud and tumbled down the hill. Axel and Raynor tried to stop me, and, well . . ."

Morgan arched her brow. "I'm glad to see chivalry's not dead."

"My arm feels like death," Raynor muttered.

Brigga shushed him.

"Well, hop in. Or crawl in—whatever you can manage." Morgan opened the back of her vehicle. It was slightly bigger than Kenzi's car, and when she pressed a button near the rear window, two additional seats rose slowly from its base.

"She has a magic car," Brigga whispered.

"You mean the optional third row seats." Morgan grinned. "They definitely come in handy sometimes."

"Thanks, Morgan." I let Axel help me into the middle row. "We didn't know what we were going to do."

"How'd you end up here, anyway?" She waited for everyone to climb in, then closed the rear door and returned to the driver's seat.

"We were volunteering with Axel and Raynor's fraternity," I said. "They dropped us off here after, and, uh, didn't come back."

All of that was technically true.

"Typical Alphas," Morgan groaned. "Sorry, guys, no offense."

"None taken," Raynor waved one hand. "Most of our housemates aren't terribly motivated."

"Good to know at least some of you have some sense." Morgan laughed. "Everyone buckled up?"

I tugged the belt across my torso, and motioned for Axel to do the same. "*Ja*," I confirmed.

"Then we're off." Morgan reversed from her space, and drove down the hill that led to the freeway. Thankfully, she didn't ask any more questions. She probably sensed that we were too exhausted to do more than sit. At some point, Axel reached over and laid his hand atop mine. I turned my palm upward, lacing my fingers through his and holding on tight. I didn't think too hard about what it meant; I just rested my head lightly on his shoulder, closed my eyes, and thanked the gods he was still alive. That we all were.

For now.

Twenty minutes later, we pulled onto The Row. As we drove into our parking lot, I saw the Kappa Mu house through new eyes. It was a welcoming beacon of light after the nightmare of an evening we'd had. Axel opened the car door, and helped me hobble out of the vehicle. I leaned on him as my knee sent a fresh surge through my leg. *Ouch.*

"Are you guys sure you're okay?" Morgan asked as she locked her doors. "I can take you to a pharmacy if you need some hydrogen peroxide for that cut, Raynor."

"I have supplies to treat him back in our room," Axel said. "But thank you, Morgan. You saved us a lot of grief tonight."

"No worries." She raised one hand in farewell and headed toward the house. "Don't party too hard tonight—you all look like you could use some rest."

"I'm not partying at all," Janna said once Morgan had gone inside. "I'm going to bed."

"Me too." Brigga yawned. "We can regroup and strategize in the morning."

"Sounds good." Raynor wrapped his arms around Brigga. "Thanks for saving my arm."

"I just pulled out the blade—Axel's going to have to treat it." Brigga shuddered. "Good luck."

Axel rolled his eyes. "He's seen worse."

"Says the guy who *doesn't* need his skin sewn." Raynor groaned.

"You'll be fine. Go back to the house and boil some water," Axel ordered. "I'll be there in a minute."

Raynor released Brigga, and turned toward the fraternity. "Pray for me, ladies."

"May the goddess Idunn grant you the wisdom to endure your healing in silence," I said.

"You are no help, Ingrid. None." Raynor waved over his shoulder as he marched reluctantly across the lawn.

"Good luck, Raynor!" Brigga called as she and Janna stepped inside.

When the door clicked closed behind them, I turned to Axel. "You'd better go heal him. It looks like a pretty bad cut, and Odin only knows what kinds of germs live in that frat house."

"I will. But first, there's something I've been waiting a long time to tell you." Axel slid his hands down my arms. Tingles rippled across my flesh as he pressed his palms to mine and laced our fingers together.

"Oh?"

Axel was looking at me with an expression I'd never seen before. It was gentle, and fierce, and vulnerable and determined, and . . . my gods, what was he going to say?

My breath hitched as Axel's eyes slid down to our entwined hands. His shoulders expanded with his inhale, and nerves pinged through my body as our chests touched. My heart pounded with such ferocity, I was sure he could feel it through the thin fabric of his shirt. His eyes moved slowly up my body, and when they locked in on mine, they bore a clarity I'd rarely seen in him. He parted his lips, and the flutters in my belly leapt into action. I was simultaneously exhilarated and terrified.

I hope we want the same thing.

"Ingrid," he said gruffly. "I've wanted to say this for a while. But I wasn't sure how you felt, and frankly, I'm still not. But I'm beyond caring. Life can be unpredictably short—especially our lives, and especially right now. And if, Odin forbid, anything were to happen to me, I need to know that you're aware of . . . of how I feel for you."

My heart thundered in my chest. "And how is that?"

Axel's eyes softened. "From the moment I first laid eyes on you, I knew you would be the end of me. You have a fire unlike any I've ever seen. Even in the worst of circumstances, your determination to fight your way to a better life took my breath away. And as I got to know you, and that ferocity evolved from a desire to protect only yourself to a need to protect your entire clan, my respect for you grew. You're the strongest woman I've ever met. The only woman strong enough to call me on my *dritt*. You challenge me in ways I never dreamed possible, and I never want to stop being the thorn in your side. Unless I can become the man who pushes you to be your best self, the same way you've pushed me."

"Axel," I said softly. My breath caught as he lowered his forehead to touch mine.

"I care for you a great deal, Ingrid Tirsdatter. I have from our very first meeting, and that feeling has only grown with each day I've gotten to spend with you. If you'll allow me, it would be my honor to court you. Hopefully one day, I'll earn your affection in return."

"You already have it," I whispered. "I didn't want to —believe me, I *did not want to*. But somewhere along the way, I fell for you, too."

"I knew it." Axel's dimple popped. "Then you won't mind if I do this."

He released one of my hands and brought his fingers to my face. Lifting my chin with his thumb, he slowly guided my mouth to his. Heat shot from my lips straight to my belly, igniting a flight of butterflies that flapped a frantic rhythm. I reached up to stroke his beard with my fingertips, and as I tilted my head, Axel deepened our kiss. His tongue swept lightly along my bottom lip, and a fresh wave of warmth coursed through me. He released my chin to slip his hand along the back of my head. He tugged lightly on my tangle of curls, angling my head just enough that my lips parted in a sigh. Axel seized the opportunity, exploring every corner of my mouth like the conquering assassin I knew him to be. His kiss was demanding—possessing. It left me with no doubt that a life with Axel would be thrilling and exhausting and exhilarating and *intense*.

I wouldn't have wanted it any other way.

When I finally pulled back, my breath came in ragged gasps and my hand had somehow worked its way under Axel's singed shirt. My cheeks heated as I tried to free it, but Axel didn't release me from his hold.

He rested his forehead against mine, and stared into my eyes. "You okay, shieldmaiden?"

"Never better." I exhaled. "You?"

"Very much the same." He pressed his lips to my cheek, and leaned back to assess me. "But you should probably head inside. I don't want you getting written up."

"Curfew's not for another . . . I have no idea what time it is," I admitted. "And I don't care. I'm perfectly happy right where I am. Lexi can just deal with it."

"Agreed. But one of us has to exercise self-restraint. And Raynor deserves a medic with a *reasonably* clear head."

Oops. I'd forgotten.

"Give Raynor my best." I reluctantly removed myself from Axel's grasp. He slipped an arm around my waist, and helped me to the house. The pain in my leg had already diminished significantly. I hoped a good night's rest would put me back in fighting shape.

Odin knew, I needed to be.

"I'll see you in the morning?" I asked as Axel guided me to the door.

"You will," Axel confirmed. "And every morning after that."

Warmth blossomed in my chest as I placed my hand on the doorknob. Before I slipped inside, I stood on tiptoe to kiss Axel one more time. It took every ounce of control I possessed to pull myself away.

"Until morning, shieldmaiden."

"See you, Andersson."

I shut the door behind me, and pressed my back against its frame. My smile stretched from ear to ear as

I closed my eyes, and committed every detail of the last ten minutes to memory.

Axel Andersson, easily the most incredible specimen in the history of Valkryis, was mine. He'd chosen *me* to fight alongside—to build a life with. The future was ours to write.

Now all we had to do was save it.

The Shieldmaiden Squadron returns in
SORORITY SUBTERFUGE

Ingrid Tirsdatter is no stranger to difficult missions. As a first-year shieldmaiden, she's fought off Viking warriors, defeated the not-quite-dead, and ridden into battle atop a fire-breathing dragon. But nothing in her training prepared her for her current assignment. In order to stop a madman from destroying her home, Ingrid's jumped one thousand years into the future, moved into an elite Southern California sorority, and done everything in her power to *not* get distracted by Axel Andersson—her absurdly attractive, and extraordinarily egotistical, battle partner. So far, she's managed to keep her mission reasonably on track. But when a mysterious stranger shows up with an offer to lead Ingrid to her target, her well-orchestrated plan begins to unravel. It turns out that Ingrid isn't the only one engaged in subterfuge. If she fails to hunt down the elements that have set her enemy on his dark path, there's no telling what will become of the future . . . or the past. Ingrid and her team are in a race against time. And if they can't outrun their target, *both* of the worlds she's come to love will be nothing more than a memory.

Meet the rest of the Valkyris crew in
VIKING ACADEMY

Erik held me until my shoulders stopped shaking—whether it was a minute or an hour, I couldn't tell. The only things I knew for sure were:

1. *I was trapped a thousand years in the past, with little hope of ever going home. And,*
2. *I was wrapped in the arms of the most absurdly gorgeous Viking to have ever walked the face of the Earth.*

Maybe my old life was overrated.

When seventeen-year-old Saga Skånstad discovers an antique dagger, she's instantly sucked into a world where Vikings rule the seas and dragons roam the skies, and the only thing more dangerous than the chief who takes her captive is the rival who steals her away. The heir of Norway's most feared tribe is fierce, cold, and absolutely unyielding. With intruders encroaching upon his borders, Erik Halvarsson has little patience for the girl whose ignorance threatens his very existence. He enlists Saga in the magical Valkyris Academy, where she learns the skills she'll need to protect herself from foreign raiders and domestic terrors. But nothing can protect her from falling for the one guy in all the world she's absolutely forbidden to choose . . . or from risking everything to unlock the secrets that haunt him.

When darkness threatens Saga's new home, she must decide whether to return to the life she's always known, or fight for a love she never could have imagined. Her decision will determine a legacy—not only for Saga, but for the world she never knew she was fated to lead.

ACKNOWLEDGMENTS

To my amazing little family—you are my heart. I'm so grateful God gave me you.

To Lauren Clarke and her team at CREATING ink, who always bring out the best in our Norse crews. To Mariana, for keeping the Viking ship afloat. And to Alison, who made sure that Ingrid got her story. I couldn't do this without you.

To the readers who take these wild journeys with me. Thank you for believing in fairy tales.

To everyone with a shieldmaiden's spirit and a dreamer's heart—thank you for bringing your light to our world.

And to MorMorMa. For everything.

ABOUT THE AUTHOR

Before finding domestic bliss in suburbia, S.T. Bende lived in Manhattan Beach (where she became overly fond of Peet's Coffee) and studied Shakespeare in Europe... where she became overly fond of McVitie's cookies.

S.T.'s love of Scandinavian culture, and a very patient Norwegian teacher, inspired her YA Norse fantasy series'. And her deep love of a galaxy far, far away led to her writing children's books for the Star Wars franchise. As an experienced IP writer, she's written multiple books published by Disney-Lucasfilm Press and its licensees.

When she's not creating stories, S.T. dreams of skiing on Jotunheim and Hoth.

Learn more about the world of S.T. Bende
at www.stbende.com .